Incident at Hawk's Hill

Allan W. Eckert

with illustrations by John Schoenherr

Little, Brown and Company
Boston New York London

Author's Note

**The story which follows is a
slightly fictionalized version
of an incident which actually
occurred at the time and place
noted.**

Eckert, Allan W.

      Incident at Hawk's Hill, by Allan W. Eckert. With illus. by John Schoenherr. 1st ed. Boston, Little, Brown 1971
xvii, 173p. illus. 21 cm.

      Summary: A shy, lonely six-year-old wanders into the Canadian prairie and spends a summer under the protection of a badger.

      ISBN 0-316-21905-3 (hc)

      ISBN 0-316-20948-1 (pb)

      [1. Badgers — Fiction. 2. Survival — Fiction. 3. Family life — Fiction. I. Schoenherr, John.] II. Title.
PZ7.E1978 In   77-143718

20 19 18 17 16 15 14 13 12 11 10

COM-MO

Printed in the United States of America

*For the great joy and fulfillment
she has brought to her family
since that wonderful
sixth day of May in 1965,
this book is dedicated
to my beloved daughter*

Julie Anne Eckert

Prologue

The Indians knew this powerful, northward-flowing stream best. Closer to its headwaters, the Dakota Sioux had named it the Wooded River because of the trees growing so densely along its banks in a land where trees were scarce. The Cree Indians, nearer its mouth, named it the Murky Water, which in their language was *Winnipeg*. Then the white men came and they had a name of their own for it, rather close in meaning to the Cree name but not quite the same. They named it for the muddy color of the water. By the time this river flowed into Lake Winnipeg, some three hundred miles from its source, twenty-three major streams had joined it, each carrying its own silt deposits which, during much of the year, turned the water a reddish-brown. The white men called it Red River.

Last and largest of the major tributaries was the Assiniboine, flowing eastward from the wilderness of Saskatchewan. And where these two rivers met, the Red River became a formidable stream indeed.

A city was here now, in this year of 1870. Almost as if in apology to the Indians who had been uprooted by the coming here of white men, it had been named what the Crees had called the stream — Winnipeg — and it was the largest city for over five hundred miles in any direction. It also held the promise of becoming considerably larger in the near future.

Forty-five miles to the north of this vigorous young city was where the Red River emptied into the gigantic Lake Winnipeg. From the frontier city northward for the first thirty miles toward the lake it snaked its way through a vast rolling prairieland, a sea of buffalo grass, with only here and there little islands of low trees and occasional rock formations jutting above the grasses. And now this ocean of wild grasses had commenced giving way to a sea of wheat, for this was very fertile land, ripe for the plough and rich in the nutrients required for growing the crop which was the staff of life.

Less than twenty miles to the north of Winnipeg in this year the wild prairies were still largely unchanged. Here and there grew neatly squared fields of wheat, but mostly the gently rolling hills were still cloaked in their original garb of buffalo grass, punctuated by stark rock formations. And on one of the hills stood a cluster of buildings — a substantial home, large barn, numerous sheds and outbuildings. In many respects it was still crude and rough but, like the very face of this land, each year it was changing.

This was the farm of William MacDonald.

Twenty years ago, with his bride beside him, MacDonald had come here, generally following the Red

River down from Winnipeg. They had started out from Toronto, where so recently they had been married. Their plans had been nebulous and they knew only that they wanted to settle new land somewhere in the Winnipeg area, though neither had ever been here and they had no idea where they would finally stop. Both were confident that when they arrived at the right place, they would know it at once.

The journey to Winnipeg had been long and hard and they had tarried there for several days, masking the sharp disappointment they felt when they learned that most of the land close in to the city had already been claimed and was being farmed, especially the areas to the east and south and west of Winnipeg. To the north, they were told, the prairieland abruptly gave way to forest land which was unfit for crops, so expansion in that direction had thus far been lightest. But — and their hopes had suddenly soared — there was still some prairieland unclaimed in the thirty miles northward before the forest line was encountered. And so they had headed that way, down the west side of the Red River, and not until they were two days from the city in the vast rolling prairieland did the countryside open up for settlement.

Then, in the late afternoon of their second day out of Winnipeg, weary of walking beside their plodding oxen, they had stopped atop this very knoll to let the laboring team blow and rest from the efforts of pulling the large creaking wagon. They stood quietly, this man and woman, with their arms linked and letting their gaze drink in this lonely but appealing landscape.

They had been a handsome couple. William Mac-Donald was of hardy Scots parentage, tall and angular, his face Indian-like in the craggy hawkishness of its features, though there was no Indian blood in him. A well-educated man, his hands were heavily callused, but this had come about through choice rather than necessity; he loved land and he loved working the soil and growing things on the land. He was rather slender but there was the look of quiet strength about him. It was an aura shared by his bride, Esther. An intelligent and gentle woman, she was a head shorter than her husband, dark-haired and imbued with an attractiveness which not even the grinding weariness of this long journey by oxcart could alter. If — as well there might be — there was any fear in her breast for what lay ahead of them, she showed no sign of it. Both were aware that hardships were ahead of them, but when such bad times came, they would be met. It was that simple.

Twenty years ago it was, in 1850, that they had paused on this knoll and stood silently together while gradually the labored breathing of the oxen diminished until no longer audible. The stillness of the great prairieland had closed in around them, yet it was not quite a true silence, for always there was the faint swishing whisper of the breeze touching and rippling the knee-high grasses. There was a strangely comforting tranquillity to this place which touched them deeply and made words between them unnecessary.

It was as they had stood thus, unspeaking, that there had come a cry — a bell-clear, piercing *kreeee kreeee kreeee* — and both of them had looked up to see a magnificent red-tailed hawk circling gracefully, effortlessly, on broad outstretched wings. They had looked at one another then, William and Esther MacDonald, and still without a word passing between them they had known without doubt that this was it, that this very spot was the place where at last they would sink their roots with permanence.

On that selfsame day they had named the knoll Hawk's Hill, in honor of the large bird of prey that had greeted them. To north and south and west the prairies rolled endlessly in gently sloped hills like this one until they touched the horizon, but to the east the land angled downward into the valley of the Red River, less than a mile distant. The woods flanking the watercourse there formed a dark undulating line through the otherwise treeless land, heading for that point another ten miles to the north where they would spread out into a vast unbroken forest.

At first they had built a cabin here and cultivated only a small area, but as the years passed the cabin became a good roomy house close to a large barn, and there were other outbuildings which followed. With each nail driven, the roots of the MacDonald family became more solidly set. They had gradually acquired some sheep and horses and a good milk cow, and just as they took onto themselves the land, so too the land took them and they became a part of it, growing to love it with the fierce intensity that is the hallmark of the pioneer settler.

Even though it was a young country here, already it was steeped with a rich tradition of history. This was Indian land, or at least it still had been when first they arrived. Roving bands of Crees had then lived on these prairies, frequently moving their impermanent villages as they fished in the rivers, hunted across the plains for buffalo, netted great numbers of ducks and geese on the multitude of marshy potholes which dotted the landscape, trapped the fox, mink, beaver, otter, badger, marten and other furbearers for trade with the white men of the Hudson's Bay Company. That had changed, too. In just this score of years the Indians had nearly disappeared, moving westward with the ever-diminishing herds of buffalo until now it had become something of a rarity to see one of those great shaggy animals or one of the red men who hunted them.

The MacDonalds had come to know the history of Winnipeg almost as well as they knew their own Hawk's Hill. It was a Frenchman, La Vérendrye, searching for a route to the Pacific, who first came to the confluence of the Red and the Assiniboine in 1738 and erected Fort Rouge. But the place had been soon abandoned and before white men came here again, Canada had been lost by the French to the English. Thus, in 1806, the North West Company had come and established Fort Gibraltar on the spot where Fort

Rouge had been, and they established as well a fur trading empire. It was an empire soon to be challenged by the already powerful Hudson's Bay Company under the leadership of Lord Selkirk. On his orders, the company built Fort Douglas close by and competitive friction developed.

The Nor'westers were not as farsighted as Selkirk, who quickly recognized the potential of the land for more than merely fur. He realized its fertility and its value for settlement. Over a period of four years he brought in three hundred families from his native Scotland to settle the raw land, mostly in the vicinity of the two forts and to the south and west of them. The hardships were many but the new settlers overcame them and built a strong colony adjacent to the forts. Friction between the two companies degenerated to actual bloody warfare before at last, in 1821, they resolved their differences and merged under the name of the Hudson's Bay Company. The company, which had seized and destroyed Fort Gibraltar in 1816, built Fort Garry on the site, and it quickly became the territory's foremost trading post and settler's depot. A second Fort Garry was built in 1835 and the town which then formed around it was named Winnipeg.

And now, in this year of 1870, a great change had taken place. The Hudson's Bay Company had just transferred title of the entire territory to the Canadian government and a territorial governor had been seated at Fort Garry. There was talk that very soon a railroad would link Winnipeg with the east. When that happened, the city would virtually burst its seams with growth. A number of little satellite communities were springing up and there were many churches and reasonably good, resident-supported schools. Roads were being built and farming, rather than fur trading, was becoming the heartbeat of the economy.

For the MacDonalds, the passage of these two decades had brought about many changes. Children had come: first John, in 1854, followed by Beth in 1858, which was the same year that the Minnesota Territory, sixty miles south of Winnipeg, was admitted into the Union of the United States. Coral was born only nine years ago and in that same year of 1861 the Dakota Territory was established, also by the United States government. Finally, three years later, Benjamin had been born.

It was strange that in this period of development, when empires and governments were being established, when civilization was carving its way into the raw Canadian wilderness, the greatest problem of the MacDonald family should center around this six-year-old son.

Incident at Hawk's Hill

Chapter 1

Benjamin MacDonald was following a mouse.

The fact that he was doing so was nothing out of the ordinary for Ben; he often followed mice. For that matter, he followed birds, too, when they'd walk rather than fly, and ground squirrels and snowshoe rabbits and anything else if he got half a chance. He sometimes even followed insects. The odd thing about it all was not so much that he was following the mouse as that the mouse was evidently letting itself be followed without taking alarm and disappearing at once.

The little rodent moved along casually, stopping here to sniff, stopping there to pick up and nibble a grain of wheat that had fallen on the barn floor, now and then standing high on its hind legs to look around while nose and ears twitched delicately as it sniffed and listened. Incredibly, the boy was doing the same thing, emulating each movement of the mouse. He crawled on hands and knees a yard behind the mouse as the mouse walked along normally. Where the mouse dipped its muzzle to sniff something on the rough wooden flooring, so too Ben, when he came to that

3

same spot, would bend until his nose was at floor level and he would sniff there. When the mouse would nibble a wheat grain, Ben would also, resting back on his haunches and daintily holding the single grain in his fingers and nibbling in the same manner. At the frequent pauses in its passage, when the mouse would lift its forepaws from the ground and stand there sniffing and twitching its ears, Ben would do likewise, squatting with his feet flat on the floor, knees bent, hands held limply in front of his chest, nose wrinkling as he sniffed, head cocked to one side as he listened.

At one point the mouse gave voice to a high pitched chirring sound. Immediately, and with incredibly accurate mimicry, the same sound came from Ben, hardly any louder than that which the mouse had uttered. The small rodent cocked its head and stared at him, just as it had looked at him a dozen times before this since the boy had started following it near the barn door. Ben looked back, his own head tilted in the same way.

There was no way of saying how much further this strange little game of follow-the-leader might have gone had there been no interruption. But then, annoyingly, feet clumped heavily near the doorway and the familiar sound of William MacDonald's voice carried through the dimness of the barn's interior.

"Ben? Ben! I saw you come in here, so don't try to pretend you're not there. I want you to come outside."

The boy had turned his head at the sound of his father's voice and now when he looked back, the tiny

4

mouse was gone. He frowned and then reluctantly got to his feet and walked toward the door. He followed his father outside and squinted against the midmorning brightness until his eyes adjusted. Ben's mother was standing at a point about midway between barn and house, looking toward the east. They walked to her.

"He was in the barn," MacDonald commented as she glanced at them, "on his hands and knees, as usual." He sounded disgusted.

Esther MacDonald shook her head faintly at her husband and then squatted down and held her arms out to Ben, smiling warmly at the boy. He came to her without hesitation and put his arms around her neck when she gave him a brief hug. She kissed his cheek and smiled again, took his small hand in hers and squeezed it. She inclined her head in the direction of the rutted wagon road leading eastward from the farm. A few hundred yards away a rider was approaching with a dog trotting along beside his horse.

"Mr. Burton's coming," she said. "Your father saw him on the way back from Winnipeg last week and he said then that he'd probably come by in the forenoon today. He's our closest neighbor now and your father wanted both of us to meet him. We'd like it, Ben, if you'd start taking an interest in people as well as animals. And I'd like it if you'd shake hands with him like a little man. Will you do that for mother?"

Ben's glance shifted to the rider and then back to her. He shook his head once and then looked at the ground in front of his feet. Esther MacDonald sighed.

"What'd you expect," the boy's father said, irritation heavy in his voice, "a miracle? Nothing short of that's going to change him."

Esther frowned and again shook her head slightly as she stood and murmured, "Will, he's only a little child yet. Give him time. He'll be all right. It just takes time."

Now it was MacDonald who sighed, slapping his hands against his sides resignedly. "I know, I know. It's what you keep saying and I guess you're right. But it's hard to be patient. Well, let's see what Burton wants."

George Burton sat easily astride his walking horse as he neared the MacDonalds. The dog accompanying him was a huge, nondescript yellow-gray cur which gave no indications of friendliness. It was apparent that the horseman was keeping the animal at heel only with continued low threatening commands.

Burton was a very large man with a massive chest and huge hands. A dense, untrimmed black beard covered the lower portion of his face and his brows seemed abnormally bushy. Without the distracting influence of the beard and brows his nose might have been somewhat too big for his face and his chin too weak, but now there was a kind of unkempt ruggedness to his countenance that one might well have expected of the frontier type that this fur trader was. He was a man who caused discomfort in those around him because his eyes never really met those of the person to whom he was talking. It gave the disconcerting impression of shiftiness, insincerity.

MacDonald was not fond of Burton, though he had to keep reminding himself that it wasn't quite fair to make a judgment yet, since he'd only met the man a few months ago and had talked with him only twice before last week. Still, there was something about the man that rankled — a sort of bluff, insincere heartiness and forced joviality that was irritating.

The farmer had met Burton — with this same dog tagging along beside him — last week while on the way back to Hawk's Hill from getting supplies in Winnipeg. It was to Winnipeg that Burton had been heading and he seemed to be anxious to get there. MacDonald had reined in his team, prepared to chat for a while with the relatively new neighbor, and he had felt a bit miffed when Burton hadn't stopped but merely said he was in a hurry and had to get on. The dog showed its teeth at MacDonald as they passed and a deep growl had rumbled in its throat. Burton cursed the animal into silence but hardly slowed his horse, and it wasn't until after he passed that he had turned and called over his shoulder that he wanted to talk with the farmer about something and would drop by in the morning next week. It was another little thing that irked; Burton didn't ask MacDonald if it would be all right for him to drop by, but rather told the farmer he'd be there.

Undoubtedly part of the dislike MacDonald felt for this man was due to hearsay. The talk among other neighbors and in town was that Burton was a cowardly man and a bully; that he was something of a ne'er-do-well who had worked for years for the Hudson's Bay people until they ran him out for defrauding the company. As near as it could be pieced together, Burton had originally come from around Quebec somewhere and for many years had trapped on his own to the north and west of Winnipeg until his brutality and cruelty toward the Indians made it dangerous for him to travel alone in the more remote areas any more. It was why, so people said, he took the huge dog with him wherever he went. Tongues waggled with stories that the dog was a killer and that on at least one occasion it had torn out the throat of an Indian who had come skulking around Burton's camp late one night.

MacDonald strongly doubted the story, but he was still wary of the big unfriendly canine. Burton, so MacDonald was told, had quit his own trapping then and had taken a job as a grader of furs for the Hudson's Bay Company. He'd held that position for six or seven years until, almost by accident, it was discovered that all this time he had been undergrading furs to the seller and then reselling them to the company himself for a much higher figure. He had evidently stashed enough money away through such fraud that when the company fired him, he boasted that he was now going to become a gentleman farmer, and immediately he bought the old Cecil homestead — a farm about six miles from MacDonald's and adjoining it to the south. This made him one of MacDonald's closest neighbors now, though William MacDonald would much rather have seen the Cecil family stay on. Edgar Cecil had crippled himself up pretty badly, however, in a fall from his horse and had felt it was best for his family and himself that he sell out and go back east. MacDonald wished now that he had bought the place, as he'd been strongly tempted to. It was good land and the idea of having Burton as a neighbor did not set too well with him. But, of course, at that time he'd had no idea Burton was to be his neighbor. Well, it was too late now. MacDonald put the hearsay behind him, determined to do his part toward maintaining good relations with a new neighbor. And here at Hawk's Hill, with Burton already reining up and dismounting, William MacDonald smiled with considerably more friendliness than he really felt and shook the visitor's hand. The big dog, he noted, continued standing stiffly, alertly, beside the horse.

"This is my wife, Esther," MacDonald said, and was pleased to see that at least Burton had the decency to remove his hat as he nodded to her and said "Ma'am" in greeting.

"The older children, John, Beth and Coral," MacDonald added, "are at school over in North Corners, but this is our youngest, Benjamin."

"Benjamin, eh?" Burton said. He smiled broadly and seemed on the point of reaching out for the boy and saying more, when the dog suddenly lunged forward at Ben. It happened so quickly that everyone was taken by surprise.

"*Lobo!*" Burton snapped. He snatched at the dog as

10

it passed him, but missed. Lobo came to a stop just in front of Ben. His lip curled back, exposing yellowed teeth, and a hair-raising growl left his throat. And then, taking them just as much by surprise, the dog's hackles abruptly lowered and the low-slung tail wagged ever so faintly as a thin, almost inaudible whining replaced the growl.

Ben had shown not the slightest trace of fear. As the dog approached him he left his mother's side and advanced to meet the animal. When Lobo stopped, Ben dropped to all fours and an identical whining sound left his own throat. In this position he was so much smaller than the dog that he had to look up to Lobo and now, completely oblivious to the people around him, he craned upward to put his own nose close to that of the dog. Lobo whined again, but this time a sound deeper in tone and of a different quality. Immediately Ben responded with the same whine.

The entire little tableau had all happened in a matter of seconds. Burton had paled, but now he reacted and strode forward, took the dog by the scruff, and virtually hurled him back toward the horse, commanding him to "Sit! Stay!" When Lobo obeyed, the bearded man turned his attention back to the Mac-Donalds.

"Lord A'mighty, I'd not've believed it!" he said wonderingly. "Lobo ain't never let nobody but me get so close to 'im. He's been taught to be mean. I swear, it skeered me half t'death. Thought sure to God he'd grab the boy's throat when the li'l feller stuck his head up like that." He shook his shaggy head and looked at Ben, who was standing up again but still looking at the dog. "Wouldn't give no bets he'd've had that much sense, but I reckon Lobo must've knowed the chil' was jus' hardly no more'n a baby. How old is the boy, three?"

MacDonald, not fully recovered and a trifle pale himself, said tightly, "He's six."

"Six!" Burton was taken aback, and with reasonable cause. Physically, Ben really did look far more to be only three or four years old rather than six. Not only was he unusually short for his age — not very much over three feet tall — he was also slight. Burton strode over toward the boy and stood looking down at him, his own massiveness underlining the extreme runtiness of the child.

"Six!" he repeated, grabbing Ben up under the arms and raising him high. "By Henry, boy, you ain't nothin' but a li'l ol' stick wearin' clothes."

He bounced the boy a time or two as a man does when estimating the weight of an object and then shook his head and added, "Yessir, this young'un don't weigh much more'n most of the growed-up badgers I've h'isted an' not nigh as much as the beavers."

The stench of the big man sickened Ben and the liberties he was taking frightened him, but though he squirmed unavailingly to get free, he said nothing. The nearness and strength of this stranger, his unwashed odor and the booming resonance of his voice was terrifying to one so small. He increased his efforts and they bore a strange kinship with the desperate struggling of a wild animal. William MacDonald's expression was more strained than before and he seemed on the verge of interceding when the trapper put the boy back down on his feet and then slapped his thigh and laughed loudly as Ben raced away to disappear inside the nearby barn.

Without pause Ben scaled the ladder to the loft and partially buried himself in the hay along the front wall. He peered down at the adults outside through a wide crack in the wall planking. George Burton was still laughing, but the sound abruptly cut off as he noted that neither William nor Esther MacDonald was sharing his amusement.

" 'Pears I skeered the l'il feller some. 'Pologize for that." He didn't sound in the least sorry, but he went on, "Didn't aim t'give the boy no fright. Jus' wouldn't've believed the way he an' Lobo got together right off. By grab that chil' *talked* to Lobo. Yessir, he actually talked to 'im. Now where'd he learn that?"

Esther MacDonald spoke up. "Ben likes animals," she said. "All animals. And it seems that animals like him. He plays with all the animals around here. They seem to know he won't bother them."

"Not wild ones, too?" Burton was skeptical.

"Well, yes." Esther looked as if she wished she had said nothing at all, but she went on, "They're not afraid of him, either. He gets fairly close to them."

"Talks to 'em, does he?"

Esther was uncomfortable and though she made an

13

attempt to sound flippant, it didn't come out that way. "Well, he imitates the sounds they make, but . . ." She let the sentence die.

Burton clucked his tongue. "Talks to critters!" he said, more to himself than to her. Then he glanced toward her husband and added, "But six years old, y'say? Couldn't've believed it if you wasn't his own pa. No sir, he jus' ain't nowhere near big enough for six."

"He's six," MacDonald repeated shortly. His manner was less cordial than before. "He's small, but he's six. He's shy. Too shy, I'm afraid, but he doesn't get to see many other people besides the family. You said you wanted to see me about something?"

"That's right, McDougall, I was wonderin' ——"

"MacDonald," the farmer said tightly, "not McDougall."

"Well bless me for a dumb Injun," Burton said, slapping his thigh again and shaking his head. "Sure looks like I started out on the wrong track here. Now I 'pologize again — to you an' the missus both. What I come for, Mr. MacDonald, I was wonderin' if you do any trappin' on your land."

Thawing only a little, MacDonald shook his head. "No," he said, "we just farm. Mostly wheat and a few vegetables. Raise some sheep, too. Why?"

"Well sir, I was wonderin', us bein' neighbors now an' all, an' you not doin' no trappin' your own self, I was wonderin' iffen you'd mind I sorta let my string of traps wander over 'cross your land from mine."

MacDonald was surprised. "I'd heard that you were going to be farming now."

"Been a-tryin' it, sort of," Burton replied, grimacing, "but it don't much seem like as how I'm cut out t'be the farmer type. Reckon I'm jus' too set in my ways. Oh, I 'spect I'll keep on tryin' a mite, but it sure ain't gonna be as much as ol' man Cecil was a-growin' there. Dunno how one ol' man could've done so much. Anyhow, I got me a misery in my back that don't much like farm workin', so I'm reckonin' I'll jus' live offen what I been lucky enough t'put away, plus whatever extry I can get offen what I trap roun' here. Won't be trappin' like when I was younger an' more able, but mebbe in a twenty-thirty-mile circle I'll get me a fair 'mount of skins. It'd sure help out iffen you won't mind my runnin' 'cross your land some."

William MacDonald did not answer at once. He considered the request carefully. He liked Burton even less now than before and his immediate reaction was to refuse him. Esther, watching him closely, said nothing. At length he gave a vague nod.

"I guess," he said, speaking slowly, "it won't make any difference to me if you run your trap line over my land. I wouldn't want you to put traps anywhere close by, though, where Ben might stumble into one and get hurt."

"Well now, that's right neighborly of you. Yessir, it truly is. Don't you fret none at all 'bout that li'l feller mebbe gettin' hisself caught in any of 'em. No sir, I 'spect I ain't gonna make no sets prob'ly nowheres

15

nearer'n a couple miles or better from the house here. That set all right with you?"

"Yes, I suppose so, provided they're not any closer than that." MacDonald paused and then added with ill-concealed reluctance, "I'm forgetting my manners. Will you come in for something to eat and some cool water?"

"Sure did pick me a fine neighbor, I did." Burton's laughter boomed out again. "I thank you, but no, I guess me'n Lobo here'll get on. Got things t'do. It was a real pleasure meetin' you, ma'am." He dipped his head at Esther. "I sure ain't one t'forget a favor done me like this."

He bobbed his head at MacDonald, too, turned and stepped back and then raised himself smoothly into the saddle. "Lobo, come!" he commanded, then nodded a final time at the couple, yanked rather too hard on the reins to turn his mount around and cantered off down the wagon road. The big yellow-gray dog kept pace easily.

William and Esther watched him go and she spoke softly, without looking at her husband. "Do you think you should have? I mean, after all the bad things we've heard about him? I don't like him, Will. He . . . scares me."

MacDonald shot a quick look at her and shook his head. "Just the result of gossip. I never yet have condemned any man on the basis of what people say about him, and I don't intend to now. A man has a right to be judged by how he acts, not by how some-one may have *told* you he acts."

Esther flushed slightly but met his gaze directly. "I'm not basing how I feel about him on gossip. I just didn't like him. Or his dog. In fact his dog scared me to death. I think that animal would tear you apart at the first opportunity. Furthermore, I certainly didn't like the way he snatched Ben up. I didn't think you would, either."

"Well, you're right, I didn't. But . . . well, maybe it was a little improper for him to do it, honey, but he was just trying to be friendly. And he apologized for scaring Ben."

MacDonald sighed and shook his head. "For that matter," he continued, "I've had Ben act almost as afraid of me, so I don't see how we can hold that against Burton." He paused, but when Esther made no reply he went on. "As for letting the man trap across our property, I can't see what it'll harm. He couldn't get very much right around here. The only beaver we have are way up in the wooded north section in Wolf Creek. Maybe he'll get a marten or an otter or two over there as well, but," he indicated the surrounding prai-rie with a sweep of his hand, "he's not apt to get much out there. I suppose he might pick up some wolves or some coyotes and foxes around the prairie dog towns, and he's apt to get some badger there, too, but I don't see that that's any loss. As a matter of fact, I wouldn't mind seeing him get rid of some of the badger. You know as well as I that we've lost two horses since we've been here because they broke their legs in badger holes."

"That's true," Esther admitted. "Oh, I suppose I'm just being silly, but somehow I took a very strong dislike to that man. And his dog."

"Can't say I'm particularly fond of him or the dog either, but he wasn't asking much, Esther, and the least we can do is to start off being good neighbors. He may be living here a long time and there wouldn't be much sense in commencing an unfriendly relationship with him right in the beginning over something as minor as this."

He put up a hand and cut her off as she started to speak. "I know, I know. You're still thinking about how he snatched Ben up and scared him, but there wasn't anything to that and if Ben was scared it was more his own fault than Burton's. It seems to me that he should have been much more afraid of the dog than the man. It was just plain stupid for him to get down on his hands and knees like that in front of such an animal." He shook his head disgustedly. "I don't know what we're going to do with that boy."

"Will, don't talk like that, please." She touched his arm gently. "Ben's just shy with people, you know that. He's spent his whole life so far right here on Hawk's Hill. He'll open up and get over it once he starts school next September. You'll see."

MacDonald smacked his fist angrily into the palm

of his other hand. "No, all along that's what we've been telling ourselves, but it's more than just being shy and it's time we faced up to it. Esther, something's wrong with Ben, more than just his being so small and shy. Why won't he talk, except just now and then to you or maybe to John? Why is he always going off by himself somewhere, all quiet and acting sort of frightened of us all the time, instead of joining in with the family when we do things? Esther, he's six years old now! He's been like this since he could only crawl around, and ever since he was four we've been telling each other that he'll come out of it pretty soon, but he hasn't. And I don't think school's going to help him any. There's just no communicating with him. How can he change any if he won't listen and he won't talk to anyone and if he won't do anything except act like he's scared to death all the time?"

"But, Will, he's so small."

"Exactly the point! He's so small that how do you think he's going to respond when next fall comes and we send him off to school at North Corners and every child in his class — to say nothing of those in the upper classes — will practically tower over him? Esther, the boy only weighs a little over thirty pounds. He should weigh fifty or more! He only stands shoulder high to normal children his own age and —"

"William!"

The word had slipped out unconsciously and Mac-Donald was immediately contrite. "All right," he said

19

hastily, "I didn't mean that. I meant that the normal
... the *average* children his age are so much bigger
and ..."

He suddenly slapped his hand to the back of his
neck in exasperation. "Oh, what's the use of trying to
fool ourselves? He isn't normal, Esther, and we both
know it, whether or not you're willing to admit it. He
not only isn't normal physically, he's not normal mentally, either. Look how he acts toward animals. And
for that matter, look how animals — *wild* animals as
well as farm animals — act toward him. Even they can
sense that he's different. Look at how that mean dog of
Burton's acted. We've just got to face facts and admit
to ourselves —"

"No!" Esther interrupted, her voice shrill, unnatu-
ral. "No, I won't listen to that, Will. I won't! He's
small, yes, and he's shy and quiet, yes. But William
MacDonald, you listen to me, our Benjamin is *not* ab-
normal. What he needs is our understanding and our
love and help, not condemnation and despair."

She moved around to stand in front of him, hands
on hips, and continued, "You complain that sometimes he looks at you with fear. I know he does, I've
seen it, and it's a knife to my heart when it happens,
but have you ever stopped to wonder why? Do you
ever try to talk with him?"

Now it was she who cut him off as he began to
object. "Wait. I said talk *with* him, not *to* him. Do you
ever try to understand him? Do you ever give him the

opportunity — the opening he needs — to talk with you? When have you ever really listened to him?

"When you speak to him — and it's rarely that you do that," she went on, "you give him orders, commands! You stand there looming over him like some giant with your hands locked behind your back — you never try to touch him! — and demand that he do this or that or the other. Do you ever make *any* effort to get down on his level, even a little? When was the last time you squatted down or even bent over when you talked to him? When was the last time you held out your arms to him? I could count on one hand the times you've picked him up since he's been out of his crib. When was the last time you complimented him for *anything*, regardless of how trivial an achievement it might have been?"

Rarely had William MacDonald ever seen Esther angry at anyone and never before had she been truly angry at him, but she was now and it was a shock to him, holding him speechless in his surprise, and he wasn't even sure how it all began. Her eyes were still flashing and though she was fully a head shorter than he, she stood indignantly before him and he felt dwarfed by her onslaught.

"What," she continued, "have you ever given of yourself to Ben? John MacDonald is your son, but he is not your only son, Will. Benjamin MacDonald is your son also. Isn't there just a little of that love you have for John left over to share with Ben? Can't you treat him a little more like you treat Beth and Coral? Ben is just as much a part of the family — as much a part of *you* — as the other three!"

She stopped abruptly and put her knuckles to her mouth and lowered her head. Her shoulders shook with silent sobbing. Self-consciously William moved to her and put an arm around her and she buried her face in the front of his shirt. They stood like that for several minutes and then she raised her head and looked up at him. The points of anger had left her cheeks, her eyes were reddened, and when she spoke again, her voice was on a more normal plane.

"Will, you've talked about how he shrinks from you, how he sometimes looks at you as if he fears you. Yes, I've seen it, but I've seen something else that you haven't. I've seen him look at you when you didn't know he was looking and there's been a look of yearning on his face that could break your heart. I've seen him follow you when you didn't know he was there, trying to do what you do, trying to be like you. And I've seen him sit by himself and cry."

Her voice broke but she brought it under control and went on. "You point out the way he acts toward animals and they toward him. I don't know why, any more than you do. Why should a wild creature let Ben come to him, even touch him, when at the sight of one of us it runs to hide? I don't know. But isn't it just possible that somehow these creatures sense his loneliness, his helplessness, his total lack of threat to them? And isn't it possible that he feels an empathy with them? Couldn't it be that he senses they, like he, are absolutely powerless before us? I don't know, Will, maybe that's silly. Maybe there's some other reason. But whatever is the matter, we just can't shake our heads and give up. It's up to us to give him all the love and help he needs."

Still MacDonald said nothing, not knowing what to say or how to say it; embarrassed because he knew what she said was true. Esther rubbed her cheeks dry with the heel of one hand and started toward the house.

"I promised the children I'd bake them a pie for tonight. I'd better get busy with it."

After a moment MacDonald followed her.

When both of his parents had disappeared inside, Ben withdrew from the crack in the planking of this loft wall where he had been watching and listening ever since running away from Burton. Unconsciously his hands came up and touched his armpits where Burton had gripped him in order to hold him up. He shuddered and frowned. Even before the man had alighted from his horse, Ben had disliked him. It was a feeling that had quickly expanded into a deep loathing. The very smell of the man, though Ben's parents had shown no indication of noticing it, had nauseated him. Now he stripped off his shirt and buried it under the hay. George Burton had touched it. He was determined he would never wear it again.

He hadn't fully understood all of the conversation that had taken place below, but he had understood enough of it to know that his father had given Burton permission to trap on their land. The thought of it frightened him, even though he was not entirely sure what it meant. He had never seen a trap, but it was evidently something to catch wild animals with and it bothered him. And after Burton had ridden off, Ben knew his parents had talked about Ben himself and he had watched carefully, more absorbed by witnessing the anger of his mother than by the words being spoken. He had never seen her like that and the very fact that she, who had always been so gentle, could become so angry also frightened him.

They had talked about sending him off to school in North Corners next autumn and while, in a way, Ben wanted to go — after all, didn't Coral, Beth and John go? — still, the thought of that, too, filled him with concern. He would much rather not go. He would much rather keep to himself and simply continue as he was doing — watching and following and mimicking the animals and birds around the farm. In the company of such creatures he was able to feel not a superiority to them but rather a sense of belonging, a lack of the fear which so easily flooded him when he was with people, even members of the family.

Ben had no idea why he was so afraid of people. He was not, as his father seemed to think, retarded in his mental processes. He was, in his way, quite intelligent. He could think things through very well for his age and he retained a surprising percentage of what was taught him by his mother and the others. It was just that he kept what he learned to himself. He didn't like to talk to people. Somehow he always felt they were pushing him, trying to squeeze more out of him than he wanted to give, or else impatient with what he might have to say.

Father was the worst; he was so big and so demanding, so short with Ben and so, well, sort of *threatening*. He'd never struck Ben, or any of the other children to Ben's knowledge, but the potential always seemed to be there. Coral, closest to his own age, he liked fairly well and sometimes he even talked with her, though clearly not as much as the nine-year-old sister would have liked. But at least they shared a sort of rapport at times that superseded conversation. With twelve-year-old Beth it was another matter. There was absolutely no communication between him and Beth. She tended to exhibit a marked bossiness where he was concerned and it irritated her when he ignored her, and so he pointedly ignored her all the more. For John, on the other hand, he felt a great attraction and he often imitated what his brother did, though mostly in such a way that John was unaware of it. John tried to be good to him, to help him where he could. Ben knew it and appreciated it. As a matter of fact, he talked with John far more than with his father and he often followed John around the farm when the sixteen-year-old was doing his chores. But even with John, just as with his sisters and father, Ben still felt a sense of wariness and reserve. They were all older than he, knew all he did and more, so what was there for him to say that they would want to listen to?

Only with his mother did he occasionally open up entirely, but even then it was only when they were alone together, when the other children were at school and father out working the fields. Then he and mother could talk and she would read to him from books and explain to him, always gentle, always patient, never raising her voice to him. Without pressing him for reasons, she seemed to understand his love of animals, and she sympathized with his need to keep to himself.

Ben left the hayloft with his brow still furrowed by his thoughts. He descended the ladder slowly and walked to the door where he stood for several minutes before going outside. One of their big white hens was close by, busily scratching the ground with her feet, clucking contentedly and pecking at whatever seeds or insects she managed to dislodge. At once Ben squatted and held his arms tightly against his sides, hands under his armpits, so that his bent arms took on the semblance of wings. Then, still squatted, he sort of waddled toward her.

The hen saw him coming and paused, cocking her head. He stopped and cocked his head at her in the same way. She scratched the ground another time or two, first with the right foot, then the left, and Ben did the same. When she uttered her low, drawn-out clucking again, he mimicked the sound precisely and moved closer to her. She let him come to within a couple of feet and when he stopped there, she moved closer to him, pecked at the trailing end of the rawhide cord that held up his pants, and then began moving off.

Ben followed her.

Chapter 2

Perhaps two miles or a little more to the north of Hawk's Hill an outcropping of craggy gray rocks thrust above the new emerald green of the prairie grasses. As was common here and there in this open country, the rocks were in a jumbled pile and appeared, from a distance, as if dropped in a heap from some giant hand. One of them was apart from the rest. It sat by itself a hundred feet from the others, more rounded in outline and giving the impression that it had bounced off the pile and rolled to one side when that giant hand had dropped the others here.

Abruptly it moved, seemed to project somewhat higher than it had been, became more elongated than round, but still it gave the appearance of a rock. It suddenly moved a dozen feet or more before stopping again and the illusion that it was a rock vanished. This was a creature of flesh and blood and fur.

She was a four-year-old badger and a very large one at that. Weighing fully twenty-three pounds, she was low and broad and sturdily muscled. She was generally a grizzled-gray in color and her long fur fluffed and rippled in the light breezes that played about her. A startlingly white streak of fur originated on top of her muzzle just behind the slightly upturned nose and continued up between her eyes and over her head and shoulders, then gradually melded with the light gray of her upper back. The rest of her face was black except for a similar streak of grayish white on each cheek which ran upwards between eye and ear to the back of her head.

The big animal had been in this area for many minutes and she was studying it carefully. She had come a long way this day and the territory was new to her. Less than three miles to the west of here she had paused like this about an hour ago, but even though there was an abundant food supply there, as evidenced by the hundreds of low prairie dog mounds all around, for some reason it hadn't suited her. The big rodents could have provided a food source for her while she was, in the days to come, unable to range her normal great distances for prey, but the terrain was not to her liking and she had moved on until reaching this area of the rock pile. Her species was a populous one; inhabiting, in this year of 1870, suitable range from the Peace River in the north and the Alleghenies in the east, to the Pacific and Gulf coasts in the west and south. Preference was clearly for plains, prairies and deserts, but sometimes they were in marshy countries or woodlands and they could even be found at altitudes of up to thirteen thousand feet in the Rocky Mountains. Wherever suitable prey lived, badgers lived there too.

Perhaps a mile to the east of where this large female badger now stood was the tree-lined Red River weaving its way toward Lake Winnipeg. Southward of her was the gentle rise of Hawk's Hill and the cultured green of an expansive wheat field in the southeastern distance beyond. To north and west stretched the new green of the prairie surface, rippling pleasantly and broken only occasionally in the distance by rocky outcroppings like this one so close to her, or by cattail reeds and low willow growth around the scattered potholes. She raised herself high now, even higher than before, lifting her front feet from the ground, looking out over this sea of grass. In doing so the outlines of her body became quite distinct and she looked far less like some wayward part of the nearby rock pile.

Her legs were short but very heavily muscled and covered with a dense fur so dark brown it was almost black. Her feet were huge and all four of them — but especially the front — were armed with powerful curved claws which were surprisingly long. She looked something like a little bear in body structure, but her stance as she raised herself like this was decidedly weasel-like. In truth, she was a member of the weasel family — the second largest member of that family, with only the wolverine being larger. And, like all the members of that family, she was largely carnivorous and a fierce predator.

She was searching for a place to build a den, and her selection of this particular area had come only after re-

jection of numerous other possible sites over a course of a dozen miles or more. Soon she would be bearing young again and experience had taught her that the care of these offspring would limit her ability to travel great distances for prey. The prairie dog town only three miles distant would not be too far away for her to take advantage of it, and the fat, blacktailed residents of it that she would catch would help sustain her during this restricted period.

Overhead a wheeling hawk shrilled four times in succession and she tilted her broad-skulled head to look at it. Her ears were round and furry, black outside and white on the inside. The one on the right side of her head had a distinct notch on the top curve of it, but this was her only visible scar. The ears were set quite low on her head and she possessed a keen sense of hearing.

The hawk caused her no alarm. Few wild creatures did any more, now that she was fully grown. In her own younger days she could have fallen prey to coyotes, wolves, bobcats or lynxes, possibly even to an eagle or a great horned owl, but such peril was now long behind her. At present the largest lynxes would leave her alone and even roving packs of wolves or dogs would hesitate to tackle her because, despite her bulkiness, she was swift and ferocious in both offense and defense and never an adversary to be treated lightly. What's more, she was without fear; if she could escape without fighting, she always chose to do so, but if battle was inevitable, then more often than not it was she who would launch the attack with dreadful fury.

But she knew well that her young ones, when they came, would be vulnerable until they had grown larger and perfected their own defenses. Until then, this very topography would help protect them. Not only was prey reasonably close at hand, but should a young one happen to be surprised away from the den by some predator, the emergent rocks so close by would make an adequate temporary refuge.

Satisfied with her inspection of the area, she dropped back to all fours and began moving about in an ever-widening circle, her nose close to the ground. The skin covering her low-slung body was loose and the grizzled hair of her sides hung straight down, nearly hiding the stubby legs. Thus, she seemed almost to flow across the ground rather than walk, and there was a peculiar grace in her movements.

Abruptly she stopped and instantly began to dig. With incredible speed those powerful, oversized front claws tore at the ground, at first ripping up clods of soil held together by the roots of grasses, but soon getting below that level to where the earth simply crumbled at her tearing. In moments her head and shoulders were no longer in sight. The thick dark tail, only four or five inches long, lashed back and forth with her exertions as she dug. In only a moment more the hind feet began helping, not only doing some digging but also lofting far into the air and away from her the dirt unearthed by the front claws.

It was by no means as fast as she could dig, and yet in less than two minutes only her rump still showed above ground and the dirt flying out from beneath her had become a veritable hail. She dug slantingly and somewhat spirally downward, and when the hole became too deep for her to thrust the debris to the outside, she would back up speedily, using all four feet to push the piled earth behind her until her rear was once again above ground level and she could thrust it away.

Three times during this early part of her digging she paused and came to the surface to stand on her hind legs to her full height of thirty inches, peering around her. Twice she saw nothing to attract her attention, but the third time she stared for several minutes to the westward, watching an animal seventy yards or so distant as it moved casually along.

She gave voice to a low but far-reaching chatter and the animal stopped, stood upright himself and echoed her call. It was another badger — her mate — who had followed her here to this area. He was very similar to her in both size and color. Though he would not assist in the den-building, he would remain in this general vicinity and when the proper time came, after nursing was completed, to bring actual prey to the young, he would help in the hunting of mice and ground squirrels and ground-nesting birds. After another brief chatter, the female reentered the hole and resumed her furious digging.

The energy she expended in this excavating was enormous and it seemed her strength would have to give out and she would need to stop and rest; but her pace in the digging did not slacken and she showed no outward indication of weariness. Ever since she had begun digging a strange wheezing sound had issued from her, as if from asthma, and this was accompanied by a series of soft growls and gruntings. Downward she continued, grumbling to herself as she went, until she had reached a depth of about five feet. Here she leveled off, but her digging continued unchecked.

Time after time she backed to the surface, thrusting along behind her the soil to scatter it at the surface. Instinctively she knew precisely when she had dug just enough so that it was not too much of a burden to push it out, yet not so little that she was wasting effort. And surprisingly, although already she had thrown outside a large volume of soil, there was little sign of it and no mounding of the excavated earth, as was so clearly evident in the prairie dog towns. The hind legs not only thrust the soil out behind but they sprayed it over a wide expanse and it fell between the grasses and did not cover the grass in any one spot. When digging for prey or to escape from danger, or even just to make a temporary den for herself, she would not take such care or expend such added effort, but simply let the dirt pile up in a huge mound adjacent to the burrow. Now, however, instinct told her that to leave such a mound would advertise her presence and possibly endanger her young ones soon to be born here, and so the scattering of the earth was cleverly and effectively accomplished.

From the point where she had leveled off, she continued digging her tunnel for another ten feet. Then, though her digging continued, she was no longer moving forward. Rather, she was hollowing out a large chamber for the den area, and still backing the excavated earth to the entry to disperse it. By nightfall she had completed this first part of her den construction. The entry hole was oval-shaped, ten or eleven inches high, nearly a foot and a half wide, and well concealed; from even just a few yards away the entrance was difficult to make out. And at the end of the fifteen-foot tunnel, the den chamber was now a domed, circular room about four feet in diameter and three feet high.

She emerged from the hole then and moved away from it through the grasses. About thirty feet from the entry she paused and shook herself vigorously, sending little bits of earth flying off that had fallen into her fur. She began to move again and suddenly darted off with deceptive speed to one side. She pounced and there was a faint piercing squeak that died at its peak as she captured a meadow vole and crushed it in her teeth. In several gulps she had chewed it up whole and then swallowed it. After licking her muzzle briefly, she continued in the direction she had been heading. When she stopped again she was fully fifty feet from the entrance to her burrow and again she began without hesitation to dig.

This burrow went down more slantingly than the first and she had already tunneled some eight or nine feet through the ground before she reached a depth of five feet below the surface and leveled off. Again she worked steadily, wheezing asthmatically with each breath, grunting and growling and mumbling to herself continually, chattering rather angrily whenever she encountered a small rock. Such rocks were not pushed out to the surface with the dirt; instead, a hole would be dug in the side of the tunnel until it was big enough to accommodate the rock, whereupon the rock would be shoved into it and packed firmly in place with moist soil.

This tunnel was very straight and quite long. As she reached a point about forty feet from the entry, the dirt in front of her suddenly collapsed and she had broken into the main den chamber. It was an incredible feat of engineering and, as always, unerringly accomplished. She was very tired now and her heavy wheezing continued long after the digging was finished; but she had built a very safe den with a short easy-access tunnel for normal usage and a long escape shaft in event of emergency.

More than half the night was gone now and it seemed likely that she would settle down for a long, well-earned rest from these labors. Such was not to be the case. Within fifteen minutes, by which time the wheezing had considerably eased, she was again emerging from the main entry. Without delay she began ranging about, clawing up bunches of light, dried grasses from last year that were still clustered at the base of this spring's new growth. When she had gathered a compact ball of them only slightly smaller than her own head, she raised herself high and, using her forepaws as hands, tucked this ball into the hollow of her neck and then bent her head down so that her lower jaw held it in place. Then, moving slowly so as not to drop her load, she returned to the hole. Here she turned around and backed into the burrow, with her front paws helping to hold the ball of grasses in place as well. In moments she had backed to the den chamber and was tearing the ball apart and scattering it on the floor.

Time after time she made the same trip for such bedding until, just before the dawning, the den floor had a compressed matting of two or three inches of the soft dry grasses. Again she left and this time went to the rock pile where, from the damp and shady ground close to the northern base of the pile, she gathered up similar loads of spongy green mosses. These, too, she carried to the den chamber until she had covered about half of the grass base with a lining of the moss.

And now, with the tunneling and den chamber completed, she curled up on the comfortable nest of moss and grass and slept. Quite soon now, certainly within the next four or five days, her young would be born. They would be her third litter and, with luck, perhaps it would be a litter as successful as the first had been; hopefully not as ill-fated as the second.

There had been three pups in that first litter and the raising and training of them had gone smoothly. It had been nearly twenty miles to the northwest of here, closer to where the prairie suddenly ended and a land of unbroken forest stretched to the north. Only once during that rearing period had danger threatened.

A badger's mother-love and instinct to protect her young at all costs and despite possible danger to self makes her a decidedly dangerous foe. When one of her babies, just newly out of the den after its eyes had opened, was nearly caught by a large male lynx, disaster had been averted by the female badger. Considerably smaller then than now, she had nevertheless launched a concerted attack on the much larger predator and had viciously driven him off squalling from his wounds. It was this lynx whose teeth had closed on her right ear and torn away a chunk of its edge, leaving it permanently notched. Otherwise, she had emerged from the fracas unhurt.

The three pups had matured and, with the help of her mate in hunting, she had kept them well supplied with food after weaning. Later in the summer she had taught them to hunt for themselves, and it was about this time that her mate had gone off on his own and had not returned. And finally, as winter was drawing nigh and the three pups had learned to care for themselves, she had driven them off to find their own territories and their own life.

Soon after that the female had found a new mate. She was with him off and on in the months which followed, once in a while even sharing her den with him. More often, however, she preferred being alone and she spent an essentially solitary winter in a succession of burrows she dug, never leveling off for the actual den chamber until well below the frost line, rarely using any burrow for very long and even more rarely returning to one after it had been abandoned by her. Such holes were never wasted, as they were used by a wide variety of creatures who were disinclined or incapable where construction of such a good den was concerned — foxes, rabbits, coyotes, snakes, ferrets, burrowing owls and others.

The following spring, just a year ago, she had borne her second litter in a den no more than a mile from where the first den had been, though the site had not been as prudently chosen. She had dug the new den close to a little creek — Wolf Creek — which ran out of the woods and along the edge of the prairie country. This time there had been six young ones in her litter — a rather large litter for a badger — and it had been an unfortunate time from the very beginning. Only days after the young had arrived there had come up a tremendous spring storm which lasted for three days. The creek swelled and left its banks. Suddenly water was rushing down into the burrow, flooding the den chamber. She had managed to save only two before the den was covered and even those two did not survive much longer.

Less than a week after these young ones had first begun emerging from the new den the female had dug, one of them got careless and was caught by a golden eagle, and then immediately stolen from the eagle by a pair of wily, roving coyotes. Only a fortnight later the female's mate had been killed by a bullet from the rifle of a horseman who happened along; and the last young one, after a fierce fight with a yearling wolf while his mother was off hunting, managed to escape to the safety of the den, but he was so badly injured that he died there in the den chamber without ever surfacing again.

The female had gone away after that, gradually leaving this area of tragedy far behind her as she spent the remainder of the summer preying on mice and ground squirrels, snowshoe rabbits and prairie dogs, sharp-tailed grouse and prairie chickens and other ground-nesting birds, until last autumn she was found by another male.

At first she would have nothing to do with him, but he persisted in his courtship and at last she came into season and accepted him. The mating, early in December, was successful, as evidenced by the litter she was now preparing to deliver; but winter was coming and in this far northern clime, winter can be a dreadful time. The badger does not hibernate as do the prairie dogs and many of the other creatures upon which it normally preys. Food, therefore, quite frequently becomes extremely scarce, almost nonexistent. It was necessary for the badger, during the preceding late summer and autumn, to have built up a heavy layer of fat in her body to help see her through. While true hibernation does not occur, activity tends to slacken greatly and the large animal remains underground sleeping much of the time and often not appearing on the surface for weeks during the coldest weather. The gestation period for badgers is only six to eight weeks and, since her mating occurred in early winter this would mean the babies ought to be born in February. That, however, would indeed be a harsh time to bear young and so nature has therefore seen fit, once fertilization has taken place, to retard the development of the badger embryos for the first two to three months.

And so now, with this month of May already a week old, it was nearing time for the female to bear her third litter. She might have as many as seven babies, or as few as only one; but whatever the number that were born to her, she would endeavor to protect them against man or beast in every possible way, even should it be at the cost of her own life. And with luck, perhaps these young ones to come would live out their full life-span of around fourteen years.

Then again, few wild animals — regardless of species — ever live out their full life-spans; a violent death almost always intervenes.

Chapter 3

Obviously George Burton had been doing a lot of talking about the boy who talked with animals, both in Winnipeg and in the little community of North Corners, about halfway between Hawk's Hill and Winnipeg, where there was a small trading post, a church, a community school and perhaps two or three dozen houses and outbuildings. In the six weeks since Burton had been at MacDonald's a whole string of visitors had come; more in that short span of time than in all the years before. At first the family was perplexed by the attention being received. The visitors always gave one reason or another why they had dropped by to visit, but it soon became apparent that what they had come to see was Ben, not his parents. In a country and a time where diversions were few, a boy who could act and talk like animals was something to see, even if a body had to travel a far piece to see him.

It was at the tiny church in North Corners where William and Esther MacDonald finally fitted together all the little bits and pieces that had been accumulating and came to the horrified realization that Benjamin had become, at best, an object of curiosity and far more often was being viewed and discussed as some sort of monster or throwback, an animal-boy.

"I swear to you, it's true," Mr. Pollete had told a little group standing with their heads together after Sunday services that day. "Claudia and I rode out there last week and there that little . . . thing . . . was, talking to a chicken!"

Mrs. Pollete nodded in confirmation and added, "Harry's not fooling. I saw it, too. Why, the child was right there amongst the lot of them, clucking and flapping and pecking just like them. It made my blood curdle. There's something dreadful queer about that boy!"

The obese Mary Deedly giggled nervously. "Know just exactly what you mean," she said. "Horace drove us up there to see for ourselves, oh, two-three weeks ago, and sure enough there he was, sitting right smack 'twixt their old plough-horse's front hooves and talking to the animal . . . and I don't mean *our* talk; I mean he was sort of nickering and whinnying. And do you know," her eyes grew round and wide, "that old horse's ears were waggling back and forth and he was nickering right back at the boy."

"Their other children, Beth, Coral and John," interjected Horace Deedly, "why, they're just as nice and normal as c'd be. I feel sorry for them young'uns, I truly do, 'cause if you ask 'em anything about the little one and the way he acts, they just get sort of all red and flustered and don't want to talk about him. But

44

our boy Elmer, whilst we was over there, he was playing at something with John over near the barn and didn't you know, right whilst they were together, here comes that little Ben, moving along on all fours and following one of their ewes, doing just what that animal was doing — even eating grass! — and bleating just like the ewe was. Elmer couldn't even tell their voices apart. And when Elmer busted out laughing about it and asked — just as a joke, y'know — if Ben was sproutin' wool under his clothes, why John, he got real upset and told Elmer to go on home or he was likely to pound him some."

"Well, there's no doubt about it," Claudia Pollete spoke up again, sniffing at being out-storied, "the boy's got *something* the matter in his head, and I for one don't want my children around him. And," she sniffed again and tilted her head meaningfully toward the MacDonalds, who were just coming out of the church, "you'd think Ben MacDonald's folks'd have enough respect for others that they wouldn't bring a freak like that around normal people."

Practically all of the conversation had been overheard by the MacDonalds, who had been standing just inside the church door; and as they emerged, these last words carried only too clearly to them. A gently restraining hand on his arm prevented William MacDonald from doing or saying something Esther felt sure he would regret later, but her own face had gone white and her lips were a thin, tight line as she helped Ben into their buggy. Beth, Coral and John soberly climbed aboard and their father took the reins and snapped the horse into movement toward Hawk's Hill.

They said little to each other on the way home, but it was evident that an aura of sick helplessness pervaded them. In the weeks past, heated discussions between Esther and William — once virtually unheard of — had become all too commonplace when Benjamin became the subject of conversation. Esther continued to plead for patience and understanding, convinced that Ben was merely passing through a stage and that he would become more involved with his family and other people as soon as he was entered in school. William was just as pragmatically sure that Ben would not unless forced to, and ever more frequently he hinted that perhaps the boy needed to be firmly disciplined out of this phase.

Ben himself was largely unaware of the upheaval he was causing. It was not true, of course, as a fair number of residents of Winnipeg and practically all of those to the north of the city seemed to think, that little Benjamin MacDonald could actually converse with animals. But the affinity he shared with them was a truly remarkable thing, as was his uncanny ability to mimic so closely all their movements and sounds.

Even when they saw him from a distance, the domestic animals on the farm would come running to him, making their characteristic sounds, and always he would mimic them and emulate their movements and frequently he would touch them. This would often be accompanied by an odd humming sound he made which bore no resemblance to any sound the particular animal might make, but which seemed to have a soothing influence over them all.

It was not only the larger vertebrate animals that intrigued Ben. Frequently he would spend hours lying on his stomach watching the ants as they toiled around their ant hills, or he would squat on his heels and watch a caterpillar or grasshopper as it unconcernedly munched on a leaf or blade of grass.

Yesterday was reasonably representative of how he spent many of his days. He wandered off to the southeast of the house for a few hundred yards to a small pothole marsh at the foot of Hawk's Hill. There he spent over two hours watching red-winged blackbirds build their woven bowl-like nests in the reed stalks. Then, halfway back to the house, he lay on his back and watched a fine bald eagle making graceful circles in the clear blue air above, gradually spiraling higher until it became a mere dot and Ben knew that if he looked away or blinked he would lose it in the vastness of the sky. He tried to keep from it, but his eyes filled with tears from staring at the bright sky and he had to blink rapidly several times. Though he strained and scanned after that, the big bird of prey was gone and he felt a sense of sorrow in him, a strong desire to be able to spread his arms and soar along with that great majestic white-headed bird, to feel the thin air rushing past and to possess a feeling of mastery over all that lay below. Tears flooded his eyes again, but this time not tears of strain. They were a manifestation of his longing, his frustration. The flight of birds! The one significant act that he could not emulate even in the slightest degree. He would willingly have plummeted to earth in a helpless fall if just once he could soar for only a little while like that great eagle.

He turned on his side and yanked a weed spear apart, then nibbled on the newly exposed tender end. It was sweet and juicy and he loved the taste of it. He was about to get to his feet and continue home when he heard a deep buzzing and watched with fascination as a huge bumblebee droned into sight close over the grass tops and then came to rest on the ground no more than a couple of feet from his face. It walked a few inches and then disappeared into a hole just slightly bigger than its own body. In a moment it emerged, or another like it, and sailed away westward low to the grass, its stumbling buzz quickly diminishing until again there was only the sound of rustling grasses and the distant splashings of some nesting mallard and pintail ducks in another of the little potholes close by.

Ben's father often complained about these numerous potholes, pointing out the wasted land that their presence caused — land, he said, that could be used for growing crops if the water could be drained off. Ben hoped it would never happen. He loved the small marsh-fringed potholes, so abundant with life of all kinds. Here there were ducks and geese of many varieties, along with noisy squabbling blackbirds, both red-winged and rusty. Now and then he would hear the piercing shriek of an American bittern in the tall reeds and occasionally he would be able to see the big bird, though more often than not it was so well camouflaged that even his sharp eyes failed to pick it out. Once he had watched, thrilled, as a relatively rare visitor here, a great blue heron, glided in and settled gently in foot-deep water and stood silently there on its girder legs, watchful for fish or frogs or whatever prey might happen by. Often there were muskrats to see, and once, to his immense surprise and pleasure, he had encountered a young beaver migrating across the prairie, heading away from the Wolf Creek basin and seeking his own new territory.

There were times each spring, usually not long after the return of the robins, when the swallows appeared and flitted over the potholes in graceful dipping flights, skimming along smoothly and drinking daintily from the mirrorlike surface of the water without alighting. He did not always know the names of the various kinds of birds he saw, but he was keen at recognizing the differences in species. Where the swallows were concerned, for instance, he knew that there were four kinds he saw — dark green, tan, multicolored and, less often, blue — and the fact that they had names that he did not know — tree swallow, bank swallow, cliff swallow and barn swallow — bothered him. There was so much to know, so much that he wanted to learn about these creatures and no way for him to do so except by observing them. Perhaps one day he would learn what they were that he was seeing; this alone made him look forward with a certain eagerness to the beginning of school, where such things were taught. One day, he promised himself, he would know all about the birds and mammals and other creatures in this prairie world around Hawk's Hill. He had no way of knowing that his own close observation of these creatures had probably brought him more specialized knowledge of them and their ways than any formal training he was apt to receive in those classes that would be available to him in North Corners.

Thus, while Benjamin MacDonald shared a strong affinity with wild creatures, he could not actually converse with them as so many people seemed to think and as seemed so apparent from his imitating of their sounds. Rarely did any day pass that he was not out wandering around in the surrounding prairies, pausing sometimes for long hours at the occasional rock piles and even longer at the pothole marshes.

Today was no exception, and after they had returned from church and lunch had been eaten, he struck out to the northwestward down the long slope of Hawk's Hill, wading through the lush prairie growth which was already approaching knee depth. He sauntered along casually, enjoying the sense of freedom he always experienced at such times.

He was not quite a mile from the farm when he paused to watch closely as a streamlined little sparrow hawk suddenly appeared coming toward him at a height of about thirty feet, its narrow pointed wings alternately beating and then remaining outstretched to glide. Again Ben felt the yearning well up in him to be able to do the same.

The small falcon, its back showing a distinctly reddish hue as it occasionally dipped and veered, continued its approach to within a hundred feet of the boy when its wings suddenly flared and then began to beat at a much faster pace as the bird hovered over one spot. For the space of fifteen seconds it did this and then it plummeted straight downward. The grass was too tall for Ben to see immediately what the little bird of prey had dived after and so he began a slow movement forward. Inching along soundlessly this way on his hands and knees through the grasses, it took him a considerable while to get to the place where the hawk had come down. The sparrow hawk was on the ground in a small area where the grass was sparse beside a clump of low viny bushes, and it was a tribute to Ben's stealth that he saw the bird before the bird saw him.

Its tail toward Ben, the hawk was busily tearing at something clutched in its talons. Now and again it would stop to raise its head and look briefly about before resuming its feeding. As Ben moved up to within fifteen feet of the bird, he could see that its prey was a mouse. The boy recognized it immediately as one of those mice that had such long hind legs and tail and which innumerable times before had leaped away from beneath his feet in amazing hops of five or six feet, bouncing three or four times like this before miraculously vanishing beneath the matted grasses. It was a meadow jumping mouse and though he did not know the name, he knew it well from the other species of mice in this area; a delicate little rodent with startling white underparts and its back and sides a deep orange-brown, with a streak of longer, darker hairs running down the length of its spine.

The hawk had by this time eaten all of the head and much of the forepart of the body, holding the little carcass down with his feet while he tugged away chunk after chunk of the meat with his curved beak. The bird was a male and beautifully colored, with blue-gray wings and rusty-red on the top of the head and down the back and tail. On each side of its head two bands of black began at the base of its upper beak, one curving back over the eye and framing the face, the other going down through the eye and bisecting the white cheek. The breast and stomach feathers were light tan peppered with a darker brown. It was a very handsome bird.

Not until Ben was only ten feet away, barely inching along on his stomach, did the hawk see him. Instantly he wheeled about, glaring at the boy, half spread his wings, and uttered a piercing, high-pitched cry of *killy-killy-killy-killy*.

Ben grinned and immediately replied in the same way, not quite able to duplicate the high clear tone of the call, but coming remarkably close to it. The bird shook his head rapidly several times in a rather comical way and then tilted it to one side. Ben cocked his own head, repeated the call and then grinned even more.

"Won't hurt you, hawk," he said very softly. "Just want to watch. Don't worry, I won't hurt you."

He didn't move any closer, but the hawk continued to exhibit a decided agitation at his presence. For a moment it appeared he would begin feeding again; he pecked briefly, nervously at the remains beneath his feet, but the proximity of the boy was too much. Abruptly the talons gripped tightly and the hawk launched himself into the air. With the remains of the mouse trailing down below, his wings beating hard to maintain flight with the added load, he flew relatively low and in a clumsier manner than before. Disappointed, Ben watched until the bird dipped out of sight with his prey beyond some dense willow scrub on the far side of a distant pothole.

He had risen to his knees when the bird took off, and now, without getting to his feet, he crawled forward to the spot where the little drama had taken place and studied it. A few tiny smudges of blood were there, along with a bit of fur and a small fragment of bone. Ben picked up the bone and saw that it was part of the skull and upper jaw of the mouse and still contained both of the incisors. The teeth were faintly yellowish and curved and each had a long straight groove down the front surface, from root to tip. Ben hadn't known that before and he studied this peculiarity with increased interest. It was one more item to add to his ever-increasing store of wildlife knowledge.

He had lain back down on his stomach on the ground as he studied this little treasure. For a long time he looked at it from all angles and then a tiny, practically inaudible sound reached him, a vague, high-pitched little squeaking sound. Long ago he had learned that rapid movement startles wild creatures, and so without moving his head at all he merely let his eyes search the cover around him. Then he saw it and was amazed that it had escaped his attention thus far. Not more than two feet away from where the hawk had nailed the jumping mouse, cleverly concealed in a small, dense tuft of grass, was a ball of woven grasses about the size of Ben's two small fists together.

He knew immediately that this was the nest of the mouse so recently killed. He dropped the jaw fragment into his shirt pocket and then reached out and carefully dislodged the nest from the clump and held it in his hand. Very carefully he turned it over and then low on one side he saw the opening, hardly as big around as his thumb. He held the hole to his ear and his thin features softened in a smile as he heard, much louder now, the several voices of its disturbed occupants.

Placing the nest ball on the ground before him, he leaned on his elbows and gently began pulling it apart. In a moment he had it in half, exposing the little hollow inside and its occupants. There were four tiny, hairless, bright pink baby mice, their eyes still no more than tightly sealed dark bumps on their heads. They moved feebly and their tiny mouths opened to release the nearly ultrasonic squeakings.

Ben plucked them out of the nest and one at a time placed them in the palm of his hand. His pleasure at seeing them was dampened by the knowledge that now they would surely die. The expected return of their mother would never materialize and they would grow increasingly weaker with hunger until at last they simply died. It was a not uncommon little tragedy of the wilds, but still it saddened him. He wished he could save them, feed them, but knew there was no way he could do so.

It was while he was pondering the fate of these little lives in the palm of his hand that there came a crackling directly in front of him. He looked up, startled, and found himself face to face with an enormous badger, evidently as shocked as he at the entirely unexpected encounter. A heavy, malevolent hissing escaped her at once, gradually turning into a rather frightening, deep-throated growl. Her mouth opened and her lips curled back to expose a fearsome array of large sharp teeth.

Ben's heart was racing, but other than blinking a few times he did not move. Twice before he had seen, at long distances, badgers moving across the prairie and each time he had wished he could see one close up some day. Badger stories were common in the Mac-Donald household and many were the stories told at the dinner table by his father of experiences with them

over the past twenty years. Ben had always listened carefully, enthralled at the tales but never asking questions as his brother and sisters did. Even so, from what his father had said in his stories and in his answers to questions from Beth, John and Coral, the badger had become something of a ferocious villain. It was a big, tough, fearless animal which even the wolves generally left alone. It could hold a whole pack of dogs at bay and few individual dogs could match such ferocity in combat. Further, if conditions were such that it became unavoidable, the badger would attack a man without hesitation. That it could easily kill a child as frail as Ben was a foregone conclusion.

Such thoughts flashed through Ben's mind in just that first brief frozen moment of the encounter and yet, strangely, he was not really afraid. Wary, yes, and certainly deeply excited, but not truly afraid. The badger seemed to be in approximately the same state. Her hackles had risen, making her seem even larger, and her lips were still curled for a snarl, but since the initial hissing and growl, she had fallen silent with her eyes locked on Ben's.

The seconds stretched into a minute and the minute into two, then three. Still they stared unmoving at one another. Abruptly the big female badger gave vent to a short, guttural grunt. As near as he could imitate it, Ben made the same sound and his effort was so well done that the badger might have made both sounds. The badger blinked and she seemed not to be staring with such malevolence as at first. Her lips uncurled slightly and now she issued a rapid chattering sound. Again Ben mimicked it, even more successfully, if possible, than he had the deep grunt. As an added measure, at the end of the chattering he repeated the grunting sound.

A faint movement in his hand reminded him of the baby mice there. The tiny rodents would die anyway. Better a swift, merciful death than the lingering one of starvation. It was with compassion and vague regret then, rather than with maliciousness and cruelty, that he slowly and carefully moved his free hand to the other and extracted one of the mice. Between his thumb and forefinger he pinched the tiny head and felt the little animal go limp. It was the first time he had ever deliberately killed anything, but he did not dwell on the thought. Slowly, still staying on his stomach, he stretched his arm out toward the badger, the dead baby mouse dangling from his fingers. The female badger did not move except to silently show her teeth again and wrinkle her nose.

When she would not approach, Ben uttered the chattering sound once more and then flipped the little pink carcass toward her. It landed on the ground only inches before her. Instantly she bunched herself and snarled loudly again, but when the boy did nothing more she gradually relaxed. Her nose twitched at the scent of the diminutive rodent and then very slowly, her gaze never leaving Ben, she lowered her muzzle and sniffed it. With unexpected delicacy of movement, she opened her mouth and gingerly picked up the offering, then quickly raised her head again. For another long moment she simply stared at him while a portion of the naked baby mouse remained visible outside her mouth. Then that disappeared also and she chewed a time or two and swallowed.

Ben grinned and with continued measured movements he took another of the mice from his hand, pinched it in the same way, and held it out to the badger, this time inching his body forward just a little in order to close the gap between them. He grunted, chattered, grunted again. The badger held her ground and rumbled deeply in her throat, but she would make no effort to take the offering from his fingers. As before, Ben flicked it to her and this time the growling ceased and she picked it up at once and ate it. As she did so, Ben moved another inch or so closer.

They were no more than three feet apart now and the female badger seemed much more relaxed. She no longer bunched tightly to the ground in a posture of defense, no longer curled her lip and growled menacingly. When the boy held out the third mouse to her, she craned her neck a little toward his hand, but then seemed to think better of it and drew back. Still Ben held it and again her head came forward and her nose barely touched the morsel, but she drew back a second time without accepting it. Ben dropped it directly below his hand and as she leaned forward to pick it up, he lowered his arm until his fingers were just barely touching the white streak of fur running up her muzzle. She flinched and glared but did not growl.

Without really having placed his hand on her, Ben withdrew his arm and took the last mouse from his other hand. This time, after pinching its head, he cupped it in his palm rather than holding it in his fingers and offered it to her this way, his arm outstretched and the back of his hand all but brushing the ground. He chattered at her.

With somewhat less hesitation than before, the badger leaned forward and neatly picked up the offering without touching his hand. As she chewed and swallowed, Ben hitched his body forward a little more and raised his hand so that it touched her lower jaw. Her muscles tightened at the touch but she did not pull away and now, continuing the chattering sound very softly, Ben turned his hand and let it touch her cheek. Slowly he let it glide to her furry, rounded ear. She trembled as he did so and a peculiar faint moaning sound escaped her. The ear, Ben noted as he touched it, was deeply notched as if someone had done it deliberately to mark her, and he wondered how it could have happened.

She did not remain still for very long under his touch. To Ben's amazed delight she turned her head slightly and her tongue darted out, briefly licked his wrist and then vanished. Chattering once again, she turned and moved away quickly in her curiously waddling, flowing gait. At first glance it seemed clumsy, but it was surprising how swiftly she moved. Ben fell in behind her, trying to emulate the movement of her as he scrambled along on all fours. He was easily outdistanced and in another dozen feet or so he stopped and sat, feeling a pang at being unable to keep up, wishing the encounter had lasted longer.

He got to his feet and looked all around, but the badger was gone. Not even movement of the tall grass revealed which way she had gone after passing from his sight. He glanced at the late afternoon sun and made a little sound. It was later than he thought. He had been gone from home for a long while and it was time to be on his way. He had walked a reluctant hundred yards or so when he remembered the incisor teeth of the mouse which he had dropped into his shirt pocket. He felt for them, but they were gone; evidently lost while he was scrambling on all fours after the badger.

He didn't really care too much about the loss. Something wonderful had happened: he had actually reached out and *touched* a badger in the wilds. He had fed it, experienced its nearness, was awed by its size and potential menace, mimicked its voice, imitated its gait, and was even licked by its tongue. He was profoundly gratified by the experience and he reached his house still in a glow over it all.

He told no one of it at first, but they noted the change in him and wondered about it among themselves. At the dinner table, following grace, William MacDonald brought it into the open.

"Don't know what you did today, son," he said, placing a hand on Ben's shoulder, "but you must have enjoyed yourself. You've been smiling to yourself off and on ever since you came home. Did you have a good time?"

He expected no reply. At best he expected only downcast eyes from the boy and perhaps a faint nod of the head. He was as stunned as the rest when Ben looked directly at him, still smiling. He nodded vigorously.

"A good time, Dad."

The elder MacDonald was so surprised he gaped. He looked down the length of the table at Esther and she gave him a meaningful glance and just the suggestion of an approving nod. John was no less surprised at the response and Beth giggled. Coral was first to speak up.

"What'd you do, Benjy? Did you see something good?"

He looked at her and nodded again. "I saw a great big badger."

"A badger!" MacDonald had found his voice, but there was disapproval in it. "You keep plenty of distance between yourself and that animal, Ben. They're plain mean and one of them could tear a little fellow like you apart in just two shakes. Let's hope George Burton can catch it in one of those traps he's set."

Ben's smile disintegrated. He frowned and his lip trembled. He lowered his eyes and bent his head again and said nothing more. The door that was briefly opened had closed again.

Chapter 4

The big female badger did not return immediately to her den after her encounter with the boy. That she had happened to blunder into him while out hunting was an unusual occurrence, but the wind had been blowing wrong for her to catch his scent and his quietness had concealed his presence until the encounter.

More surprising was the fact that she had not immediately raced away upon seeing him. And even stranger yet was what had ultimately happened; that she had not only taken food from him, but that she had let him reach out and actually touch her. Yet in some instinctive way she had seemed to know at once that he was not a threat to her. His small size was perhaps the determining factor. In weight he could not have been more than a dozen pounds heavier than she and while his length was greater than hers, she was broader and more heavily built than he. She seemed somehow to understand that she herself was more a threat to him than vice versa, and his very defenselessness had worked in his favor.

Nevertheless, the encounter had been unsettling and

she did not resume active hunting again until she was almost a mile away from the place where they had met. The four baby mice were a delicacy to her, but they had little more than whetted her appetite. Normally she was a nocturnal animal, preferring to do her hunting by night and rarely seen, even at a distance, by man. These days, however, she was almost constantly hungry and was abroad hunting nearly as much in the daytime as at night, with much of what she caught and ate going toward development of milk in her mammary glands for the sustenance of the three offspring in her den.

In the thirty-three days since their birth they had grown considerably, but they were still relatively help- less and as blind as the day they were born. For a while yet they would be wholly dependent upon her, but within two weeks their eyes would open and they would then be ready for weaning. At that time she would begin bringing them actual prey — prairie dogs, chipmunks, snowshoe rabbits, prairie chickens, mice — and in the den they would growl and snarl over it and tug at it, have mock battles over it, pounce upon it ferociously and pretend over and again to kill it, and then eventually gorge themselves on it. At this point the female's burden would ease somewhat, be- cause as soon as the young began taking solid food, then her mate — who was still hovering in the area and occasionally seen — would also hunt to help sup- ply their ever-growing needs. The birds and amphib- ians, reptiles and small mammals he caught he would bring to the den area and drop on the ground there, leaving them for the female to take down to the pups when next she emerged or returned from her own hunting.

As these three offspring grew ever bigger, it would take the combined efforts of both parents to adequately supply their demands for food. It would be a busy time for the adults and not until mid-July, when the pups were two-thirds grown, would they finally emerge for the first time from the den in which they had been born, and at that time they would begin to accompany their mother to learn from her the techniques of hunting their own prey.

For the time being, however, she would continue to hunt prey for her own consumption and it was to this end that most of her energies were concentrated. As was frequently the case, she headed toward the biggest prairie dog town in this area; the one which began about three miles to the west of her den. Hundreds of foot-high mounds of bare earth indicated the presence of the burrows they made, but this prairie dog town, though substantial in size — a half-mile wide and about four miles long — was really quite small as such concentrations went and probably had fewer than a thousand rodent residents. This Winnipeg area was near the northernmost limits of the black-tailed prairie dog's range and the grass here was heavier and taller than the species generally preferred, even though much of it within the immediate area of the town had been eaten, torn down or trampled. Farther to the south and west, in the Dakota Territory and beyond, where the grass was shorter and much more sparse than here, the prairie dog populations were truly enormous. One such prairie dog town began in the Dakota Territory and stretched far out into the land of the Cheyennes. It was just over one hundred miles in width and fully two hundred and fifty miles in length. Within its confines lived the staggering population of over four hundred million black-tailed prairie dogs. And Texas was right now in the midst of a campaign to eradicate the species — said to number over seven hundred million there — because they competed with the cattle for food.

The female badger paused briefly on three different occasions before reaching her destination. The first time was when she flushed a sharp-tailed grouse hen from her nest. The bird thrashed off in the grass as if in great distress, emitting a peculiar clucking sound and holding one wing badly askew to give the impression it was injured. But she had waited too long to leave the nest and the badger spied the clutch of eleven eggs in a faint depression of bare ground under the sheltering grasses. She gave no further heed to the frantic bird, but went to the nest hollow and one by one crushed the pale olive, cinnamon-speckled eggs between her teeth and then lapped up the contents.

The grouse was still clucking distressedly in the grass some distance away when the badger finished. Paying no attention to her, she licked the residue of yolk and albumen from her front feet and immediately struck out westward again. It had been merely a snack that had done little to satisfy her gnawing hunger.

A hundred yards farther on she paused to sniff at the still-warm bedding place where a snowshoe rabbit had crouched. It had evidently heard her coming and fled only moments before. She wasted no time in fruitless search for it — badgers rarely attempt to run down their prey — but she did remain long enough to pull a plump rose hip from a wild rose trailer close by and munch it down as she continued her trek.

Finally, within sight of the prairie dog town, she caught a large black cricket that had imprudently leaped up directly in front of her. A flashing forepaw pinned it to the ground and in moments the insect had followed the baby mice and grouse eggs.

Pausing here a moment longer, the badger looked out over the rodent village before her. Numerous prairie dogs were moving about in the distance close to their mounds, or sitting high upon them as they watched carefully for possible peril which might appear in the form of hawk, eagle, ferret, coyote, lynx, badger or some other predator. Even as she saw them, one of the lookouts saw her and instantly issued a piercing barking sound, followed by a high-pitched *churrrr*. The speed with which the prairie dogs vanished down their burrows at this warning signal was almost comical. One of the closer ones, some distance from its burrow, ran so fast to reach it that it tumbled, rolled over, regained its feet and raced on. At its burrow it paused for just an instant to stand high and look around and then it plunged out of sight, its own barking cry hanging in the air behind it.

The badger headed toward where the last individual disappeared. She seemed to be in no particular hurry. Her own highly developed technique of hunting for these, her most favored prey, practically assured success, even though at the cost of considerable energy.

She stopped for a moment to sniff at the entrance to the animal's burrow, but then left it and began walking an expanding spiral course around the opening, grunting and wheezing occasionally. She was perhaps fifteen or eighteen feet from it when she stopped. Nothing about the surface of the ground here seemed in any way different from the surrounding ground, but at once she began an incredibly fast digging almost straight down. Through a process still mystifying to man, she had located the exact place in which to dig the least in order to reach her prey. No other animal in North America can dig as rapidly as the badger and the speed in digging which she had exhibited when building her own den was as nothing compared to her excavating now. In less than one minute only her rump and thick, dark brown tail were still above ground. Within ninety seconds she was completely out of sight, though dirt still flew in abundance out of the hole and her wheezing grunts could still be heard. Just short of three minutes from the time she began digging, she had tunneled down nearly six feet and her peculiar sensitivity had enabled her to intersect the prairie dog's tunnel only a foot or so from its den. Immediately she began enlarging that tunnel to accommodate herself and hopefully to trap the big rodent in its own chambers.

The one factor her incredible directional sense could not determine for her was whether or not the den she was angling to from the surface had an escape tunnel as well as a main shaft. If it did, as sometimes occurred, then her efforts would have been in vain and the big ground squirrel would quickly escape through a maze of interconnecting passages. If, however, the badger's estimation of the subterranean situation was correct, the den she would be heading for would be a cul-de-sac, an isolated nesting chamber at the end of the tunnel system, with no other outlet; what had been a haven for the prairie dog would become, instead, a trap of its own making.

Such was the case now. Upon emerging into the rodent's tunnel, the female badger paused in her digging to listen. Ahead, despite her own labored breathing, she could hear the trapped animal furiously digging, trying desperately to create a new exit from its chambers. Expert digger though it was, it could not begin to match the excavating speed of the badger. In seconds more the badger broke into the den and plunged into the new hole on the other side of it that the prairie dog was digging. She enlarged it as she went and a moment later there came a muffled little cry as she overtook her prey and ended its life with a powerful bite which severed its spine.

With the limp rodent in her mouth, she backed into the chamber, turned around with difficulty and then headed toward the surface in the tunnel she had dug. Only five minutes from the time she had begun digging, she was back in the open air with the object of her hunt. She dropped the three-pound rodent and shook herself, scattering the dirt clinging to her dense fur.

The prairie dog was a stout adult male about a foot and a half in length. Its tail was short and black-tipped and its body fur was yellowish-tan above and rather whitish below. It made a heavy burden for the badger to pick up and carry in her mouth, as she did now, heading toward her den.

She was still about half a mile from her own quarters, huffing and grunting with her efforts, when a powerful and intriguing odor assailed her nostrils. Without dropping her prey she paused and sniffed several times. Even with the smell of the prairie dog strong in her nose, the new odor was evident and an extremely compelling one. Had she not had prey already to bring back to her den, she would have followed this new scent to its source.

Now, however, she resumed her journey to the den and heard her offspring begin to whine with excitement almost as soon as she started down the burrow. She carried the prairie dog into the den with her and then lay down beside it. Even as she began eating it at her leisure the three pups, mewling and whining and nuzzling against her, found the engorged nipples on her lower abdomen and settled greedily to their own repast. They had not been fed in nearly five hours and they were ravenous.

The big female ate only about a quarter of the large ground squirrel and then, her stomach full and her breathing easier, she cleaned the babies thoroughly with her tongue and then lay back and slept while they continued to nurse from her. What remained of the prairie dog she would continue to eat over the next three or four days, content to relax in her den with the pups until hunger once again forced her to hunt.

Outside, as darkness fell, the same fascinating scent that had come to her nostrils, now was detected by her mate. Only moments before, he had awakened from his day-long sleep and emerged to hunt throughout the night. He was easily as big as the female, perhaps just a shade bigger, and from outward appearances seemed identical to her except that his head was a slight bit broader, his skull more massively built than hers. He was less than a hundred yards from his own den when the intriguing smell came to him and he began following it up at once.

Sardines have a heavy, oily aroma and though the male badger did not know this was what he was smelling, his olfactory sense did tell him it was fish and that it was good to eat. About a quarter-mile from where he first detected the scent he came to its source.

Had he paused, taken his time, advanced carefully, he might have detected just the faintest scent of metal and perhaps the even more elusively lingering smell of man. But the heavy sardine smell so overpowered these that he did not hesitate; last night's hunting had been poor — a couple of meadow voles and a jumping mouse — and his hunger had made him incautious. There was freshly turned earth where the smell was strongest and immediately he began to dig on the spot. Hardly had he begun when something seemed to leap from beneath the soil at him and then an agonizing pain shot up his forelegs.

He lurched backwards, snarling ferociously, only to be brought to a jerking halt and thrown to the ground when the steel trap clamped on both front legs reached the end of its chain. He shrieked and howled and tore up the ground in his frenzy to get free, biting impotently at the hard metal and time after time being thrown down heavily as the end of the chain was reached in his struggling.

The metal ring on the end of the chain farthest from the trap was securely wired to a thick wooden stake that had been driven deep into the ground so that its top had been buried in the earth. Had he been able to reason over his predicament, even though his front feet were imprisoned he might have been able to dig enough to unearth the stake and hobble away with the trap. Such reasoning, however, was beyond his capacity; he knew only that he was caught and his instinct drove him to jerk and struggle and bite at the object which held him, the trap itself.

All through the night he alternately struggled and rested, sometimes snarling and biting at the trap or even at his own imprisoned feet, sometimes lying outstretched at the very limits of the chain, panting heavily and occasionally whining with the pain the trap was causing him.

This was one of the sardine-baited traps that had been set by George Burton. He was a better trap-setter than he was a trap-checker. For two nights and the better part of two days the male badger lay helpless in his deadly predicament, his struggles weakening and his thirst and hunger increasing. So furious had the initial night's struggles been that now, in the late afternoon of the second day, hardly a blade of grass or undisturbed ground remained within the radius of the trap's chain.

The badger was on his side and appeared too weak even to stand, but at the sound of Burton's horse approaching, the animal was again lunging and tearing in his efforts to get free. When such struggling remained as futile as ever, he simply bunched himself to the ground and crouched waiting, snarling and issuing deep fearsome growls as Burton stopped his horse.

The big yellow-gray dog, Lobo, was not with him. Burton had decided he'd be more trouble than he was worth this close to home. It would not be helping the trapping any to have dog scent all over the place or maybe have Lobo get caught himself by digging after the bait. Burton dismounted and approached the trapped animal.

"Well," he muttered, " 'stead of a coyote, looks like I got me some shavin' brushes. Yessir, it purely does."

He was well back from reach of the badger but still he leaped back a few feet further when the animal lunged toward him with an awful snarl and was thrown heavily to the ground by the snubbing of the trap. There was still plenty of life in the badger and no trace of fear; only a deadly malevolence directed at this man who stood just beyond his reach.

Although Burton had a rifle in his saddle scabbard, he did not take it out. He had no intention of wasting a cartridge where it need not be used, nor in damaging a pelt with an unnecessary bullet hole. Instead, he untied from behind the saddle a stout two-foot length of mallet handle. With this club he advanced on the badger and stopped again just out of reach until the thrashing animal was so exhausted he could only lie there wheezing and glaring at his enemy.

Burton handled the club with the deftness of long experience in its use. With his viciously accurate swing he struck the badger slantingly across the crown and bridge of the muzzle. The badger stiffened and his hind legs stuck straight out and trembled violently for a moment, then relaxed. Burton did not hit him again. He had no need to. It was rare indeed when he needed to dispatch his trapped animals with more than a single blow.

With casual competence, he opened the trap and freed the badger's mutilated front legs, wrinkling his nose at the stench of the badger's musk in the area. He then tied a length of rawhide cord to those legs and lifted the animal.

"Lord A'mighty," he muttered, "iffen you ain't jus' about as heavy as that li'l MacDonald chil'."

He carried the badger to his horse and though the mount shied from him a bit at the smell of the dead animal, he managed to lay the carcass across the horse's back behind the saddle. He reached under the belly of the horse, pulled the trailing end of the cord to him and tied it snugly to the badger's hind feet, then anchored the animal even more firmly in place by tying the tail end of the cord to a small metal ring on the saddle.

It took him a little longer to dig up the stake holding the trap, but soon he was all loaded and ready to leave. This site, he knew, torn up as badly as it was and stinking from the musk released by the badger in its struggles, would be unfit for any further trapping. The relatively nearby MacDonald place was on his way home so he headed his horse toward it, figuring it would please MacDonald to see that one of the badgers that he so disliked had been caught. He had only traveled half a mile, however, when he suddenly reined in and got off his horse. He walked a few yards and then squatted down, squinting into a large oval-shaped hole slanting into the ground.

"Well, well, now," he muttered, "looky here. I

reckon I got me another badger. Yessir, big'un too, size of that hole."

He walked back to the horse and put a hand on the dead badger's back. "Ain't your den there, is it?" he said. "Nope, reckon not, the way the pilin's've been scattered. Yessir, reckon we done found us a breedin' den. With any luck, your big ol' missus'll be with you right quick."

He worked fast and wasted no motions, aware of the approaching sunset and anxious to reach Hawk's Hill well before dark. Long years on the frontier had taught him that it sometimes could be downright unhealthy to come up on a man's place unexpected after dark. Some folks got the spookies pretty easy and figured it was easier to shoot first and ask questions later.

Burton moved back away from the hole about twenty yards and stopped close to a heavy slab of rock lying on the ground. He nodded his approval and dug a hole about five inches deep and a foot in diameter. Next he got the steel trap and removed the wire from the stake to which it had been attached, then secured it to the big slab, grunting as he tilted it on edge. The rock weighed fifty pounds or more and would serve adequately as a drag. He didn't want to do any stake-pounding here as it would be apt to alert the female if she was in her den and make her carry her young away from here just as soon as he left. He knew his quarry well.

With the wire well secured, he took a flat tin of

sardines from his pack, opened it and put three-fourths of the contents into the bottom of the hole he'd made. Then he set the trap, making sure the trigger blade was well enough engaged in the pan slot that the weight of the earth with which it would be covered would not set it off, yet not so firmly that the light touch of a badger's paw would fail to trigger it. Again his experience told him when the setting was just right.

With the device set, he positioned it carefully in the hole atop the sardines and placed a large flat leaf over the pan and jaws of the trap. This was to keep dirt from trickling under the pan and rendering it incapable of being triggered. Next he donned a leather glove to mask his own scent and with this hand began sprinkling loose soil over the trap. When it was covered with a thin layer he placed the remaining sardines — except for one — directly over the trap, then continued sprinkling more dirt until the entire set was hidden. Then he scraped up some dried grasses and sprinkled them lightly over the fresh dirt and onto the wire twisted around the rock.

He popped the last sardine, as always, into his own mouth and chewed noisily as he stood up and stepped back to inspect his handiwork. He had done well; without prior knowledge that the trap was there, its existence would never have been suspected. Just as had occurred with the male badger, the next animal which dug here after the bait would be trapped by the steel jaws which would leap with great speed from under the soil to grip the leg in an unbreakable hold.

"Ain't lost the ol' touch a'tall," Burton said and then, turning, "C'mon horse. You'n me's gonna go visitin'."

Chapter 5

There was still an hour of daylight remaining when George Burton alighted from his horse before the Mac-Donald house on Hawk's Hill. The family was on the point of sitting down to dinner and, though Esther shot William an exasperated look, there was nothing to do but invite the bearded trapper to join them. MacDonald was just as irked as his wife but managed to mask his feelings reasonably well when Burton accepted the invitation with alacrity. It was still a little while before dinner would be on the table, so before eating they all came out to view the large badger Burton had killed.

Drawing his bone-handled skinning knife from its belt sheath, Burton severed the cord and tumbled the large gray animal onto the ground with a heavy thud. Only Ben, of the entire family, made no comment congratulating Burton on his catch or admiring the size of the animal. Ben simply stood back a little from the rest, his face pale and devoid of expression.

"Really fooled 'im," Burton boasted. "Got 'im by both front feet, an' badgers ain't the easiest critters t'draw to a trap, neither."

Esther and the two girls went back inside the house but Burton went right on talking as Ben's father and brother remained squatted by the badger, inspecting it.

"Kind'a hard t'figger that this critter's first cousin to a mink, otter an' marten though, ain't it? He like t'tore me apart 'fore I clouted 'im."

MacDonald merely grunted while John touched the front paws gingerly and whistled.

"Look at the size of those claws, dad. No wonder they can dig so fast."

William MacDonald nodded and used a forefinger to push the upper lip back so the teeth were exposed. One of the canines was chipped at the point and split down its entire length from gnashing against the metal trap, but the array of teeth was still formidable. Burton chuckled.

"Knows how t'use 'em too, boy," he said. "Teeth an' claws both. Don't know of nothin' else for its size, 'cept mebbe a wolverine, that's any fiercer. My dog, Lobo, he's big an' mean, but he's mighty keerful any more 'bout takin' one on. Got real careless oncet when he was jus' over bein' a pup. Tore into one that was caught by a hind leg in one of m'traps. Never in my borned life seen sech a ruckus. Ol' Lobo, he was a'comin' off a bad second best, even though the badger was hung up by the trap. Fin'ly had to step in m'self an' tap the critter on the head so's Lobo c'd chew 'im a li'l easier. Even then, Lobo needed doctorin' an' he limped round for a couple weeks after.

Now, like I say, he's right keerful. He ain't 'fraid of 'em, but he purely respecks 'em these days.''

The elder MacDonald had pulled out a few hairs from the body and was studying them closely in the sunset. ''Now this is a surprise to me,'' he commented. ''I always thought their fur was just plain gray, but it's not. Look here, John.'' As John moved in close to see, he went on, ''Notice, right at the bottom here each hair is gray, but then there's a streak of white, followed by a streak of black. Right out on the end here it's sort of silver-tipped.''

Burton grunted, oblivious of the fact that he and his comments had been thus far pretty much ignored. He went on, ''Changes color some with the seasons. The face allus stays 'bout the same, but the critter's a lot grayer, lighter-colored, in winter than in summer. This'un's sort'a betwixt an' between right now. Few weeks from now his belly'd be sort'a yeller, 'stead of whitish like now, an' his back'd be browner.''

''Come to dinner!'' Esther called from inside the house.

The three got to their feet and went to the wash stand to clean their hands, then went inside. Ben remained rooted where he was. In a moment his father's voice came.

''Ben! . . . *Ben!*''

''Go ahead and start serving yourselves,'' Esther said. ''I'll get him.'' She came outside, saw Ben still standing there and went to him. She leaned down and slipped her arm around his shoulders and hugged him.

"Ben, honey," she said softly, "mama's got dinner ready now. Aren't you hungry?"

Ben shook his head without looking at her. Esther followed his gaze to the dead badger and nodded her understanding. She squeezed him again and kissed his cheek.

"I'll put something aside for you, dear, in case you get hungry later on. You can stay outside now if you like."

She went back inside and Ben could hear her explaining to the others that he didn't want to eat and she had told him he could stay outside. For a while after that there was only the clink and clatter of tableware and scattered comments. Ben paid no attention to them. For the first time he came close to the dead badger and reached out a hand to it. The fur was coarse, yet soft but the body was cold and now growing stiff.

The badger was on his right side, the right ear hidden from view, and Ben gently rolled it over onto the stomach. He fully expected to see the notched ear, but it was undamaged. He inspected it carefully to be sure. The ear was whole, unmarked. This was not the badger he had encountered out in the prairie and a wave of relief flooded through him. He sat down beside the big animal now and began gently stroking its fur, making a little crooning sound and occasionally giving voice to a quiet chatter such as the female badger had made.

82

Conversation inside the house was by this time picking up and, though Den paid little attention to it, it was clearly audible outside. Not surprisingly, Burton was doing most of the talking and his voice rose and fell, punctuated with bursts of laughter which never quite seemed genuine.

"Ours ain't as good quality they tell me, as European badger, but good enough, I reckon. Pelt like that'un out there oughta bring in twelve, mebbe fifteen dollars. It don't make a 'specially purty fur — not like otter or beaver — but it's got uses."

"Coats?" John asked.

"Some. It shucks off the rain purty good when they tan it with the fur on. Hear tell they use some of it t'make hand muffs for the ladies back east, an' collars for their coats. Mostly used, though, for shavin' brushes. Ain't nothin' makes better shavin' brushes than badger fur."

He barked his mirthless laughter and went on, "Useta could jus' shave off the hair 'thout havin' t'skin 'em an' you c'd get eighty-ninety dollars a pound for it. Markets back east won't take it no more thataway, though hanged iffen I can figger out why not. Now they jus' got t'have a whole cured pelt. Can't see as it makes no never mind iffen they're gonna use 'em for shavin' brushes, but that's what they want. They say European badger's got even better fur for 'em, 'cause it's a li'l stiffer an' makes better bristles, but ours is still plenty good. Reckon they're using some for makin' pitchur-paintin' brushes for artists, too."

"I'm glad they're good for something," William MacDonald commented. "I've always considered them a complete nuisance. Two of my horses have broken their legs in badger holes and had to be shot. I guess they make those holes when they're hunting prairie dogs and gophers and the like. Those animals are a nuisance, too, but at least the holes are smaller and they have a mound of dirt so you can see it and keep your horse from stepping into it."

The conversation inside lagged for a little while, but Ben was still paying no attention to what was being said. The sun had set some time ago and the twilight was deepening. The gray of the badger's body seemed darker and only the white streak up its snout and over its head still seemed startlingly bright.

Lamps had been lighted in the house. There was the sound of dishes being cleared away and the conversation was picking up again. Burton's voice was unmistakable as it rumbled out.

"Ma'am, that was jus' about the best dinner ever I et. I'm 'bliged to you."

Esther's reply was inaudible to Ben, but then Burton went on. "Look here, boy," he said, evidently showing something to John.

"What is it, Mr. Burton?"

"Tooth, boy. Badger fang. Ain't ary lucky piece no better t'tote 'round in your pocket with you than a badger tooth. Most of the Blackfeet an' Sioux an' Cheyennes, they wouldn't be 'thout 'em. Figger they're powerful medicine for keepin' bad spirits away. Me, I like spirits an' I ain't never been troubled by bad ones yet, so I reckon they're right." He laughed uproariously.

"You ever et badger, MacDonald?" Burton went on after a moment. Ben's father must have shaken his head because the trapper added, "Well, you sure been missin' somethin'. Let me tell you, they ain't hardly no better eatin' nowheres. Specially the hams. They jus' purely can't be beat eat. Reckon I'd take badger hams over moose steak any time, an' ever'body knows you can't hardly get no better'n moose steak."

"Don't believe I'd much care for it," MacDonald said. He sounded as if he was tired of Burton's loquaciousness, overdone joviality and somehow insincere friendliness. His chair scraped loudly as he pushed it back and then the same sound came from the others. "Guess you'd better get to work if you're really planning on skinning the badger here like you said, Burton." He obviously wished the trapper would change his mind and go.

"Guess so. You ever skin one?"

"No. I've skinned a few coyotes and wolves, along with lots of beaver and muskrats years ago, but no badgers."

"Well, whyn't you try your hand on this one?" Burton said. "Skin 'im jus' like you'd skin a li'l ol' mushrat. Go 'head, take a whack at it."

MacDonald hesitated, but then John's voice chimed in. "Sure, dad, why not? Try it. I'd like to see you do it."

By this time they were coming out onto the porch, MacDonald carrying a lighted lantern, though the western sky was still faintly tinged with color. Ben scrambled to his feet and moved off to stop and stand quietly about twenty feet away. He watched as the men walked over to the carcass and stiffened as Burton turned it over onto its back with the toe of his boot. MacDonald set the lantern on the ground close to the hindquarters of the dead animal and then accepted Burton's skinning knife when the man extended it toward him.

As his father kneeled by the badger and prepared to slide the blade under the skin close to the body on the inside of one hind leg, Ben's eyes widened. He shrieked and rushed forward, darting between John and Burton, and struck his father's arm, knocking the knife out of his hand.

Irritated to begin with at Burton for virtually inviting himself to dinner and now for inveigling him into skinning the dead badger for him, MacDonald's anger suddenly bloomed and centered itself on Ben. Almost as a reflex action he struck out at the boy and his open hand caught Ben on the side of the head. Ben reeled backwards several steps and then fell. John moved to help him up, but Ben scrambled to his feet and raced away to the darkness of the barn, a mournful moaning sound following him all the way.

"No sense in that," MacDonald said bitterly, berating himself. "No sense at all in doing something like that."

Burton misunderstood him and he nodded. "Yep, a sprout oughtn't t'act sech a ways nohow. Good thing you clouted 'im a good 'un. Reckon iffen you give 'im a few good whalin's, you'll knock some of that queerness outa him."

MacDonald had picked up the knife again and now he glared up at Burton, no longer masking his feelings.

"I was talking about myself," he said coldly, "not about Ben. I never hit Ben before and I shouldn't have now. Not when I was mad at . . . something else. John," he turned to his older son, tilting his head toward the barn, "go after him and bring him back out with you. Tell him I didn't mean it and I want to apologize."

John nodded and strode off toward the barn, paused about halfway there and went back to the house. In a moment he came out again with another lighted lantern and then went into the barn. MacDonald was rapidly skinning the badger and there was now no conversation between himself and Burton. He slit the skin up the inside of each hind leg, encircled the genitals with an incision that joined the one leg skin cut with the other and then cut a circle around each of the hind paws to free the skin.

"Grab the feet," he told Burton curtly.

The trapper did so and while he held on tightly, MacDonald gripped the skin and pulled it down inside-out over the animal, as if it were a furry stocking being peeled off. When the carcass was bare to the front paws and head, he similarly encircled those paws with cuts and pulled the skin free from them. It was a little more difficult to free the skin around the ears, eyes and lips and by the time skin and carcass were separated, John had come back out of the barn. He no longer carried the lantern with him.

"Ben's in the back of the third stall, dad," he said. "I told him what you said, but he just shook his head. He won't come out. I didn't think you wanted me to force him."

MacDonald sighed. "All right, John, thanks. You go on back to the house now."

As the youth left them, MacDonald stood and handed the knife, handle first, to Burton. Then he picked up the skin and wadded it into a ball and tossed it to the trapper. He touched the naked carcass with his foot. "Take the carcass with you too when you leave, Burton."

Without waiting for a reply, he spun around and headed for the barn, wiping his hands on his hips as he did so. Inside the barn he saw that the lantern John had brought in was standing on the floor at the entrance to the third stall and he walked over there. The anger was gone now, replaced by a contriteness which only deepened when he saw his six-year-old son sitting in a far corner of the stall, his face buried on his knees, his little arms clasped around his lower legs. MacDonald went to the boy and sat on the straw-covered floor beside him. For a little while he said nothing. Then he reached out hesitantly with his hand to touch the boy's hair, but withdrew it before contact was made. He cleared his throat.

"Ben," he said, "you know I didn't mean it. I . . . I was angry . . . not at you . . . at Burton . . . and I just struck out without thinking. I'd never intentionally hurt you, son."

There was no response from Ben, no movement. Now MacDonald's gnarled hand came out again and this time he rested it on the boy's shoulder. He thought he felt the boy cringe, but he wasn't sure.

"Ben," he said again, "I'm sorry. Please believe me, I'm sorry. I guess I know how you must have felt. I should have realized. Will you . . . can you . . . forgive me?"

Still there was no response and MacDonald exhaled audibly and his hand slid off Ben's shoulder. He stood and looked down at his son. How small he was! And how big he himself must appear to the boy. He wished desperately that he could do something, say something, to make Ben respond, to open up communication between them, but he just didn't know what to do or say. He sighed again and walked to the stall entry where he paused and looked back. Ben hadn't moved.

"Expect your mother'll be in after a bit, son."

Esther and John were sitting at the kitchen table waiting for him when MacDonald came in. The girls had evidently been sent to bed. William shook his head as he dropped to one of the chairs. He put his elbow on the table and cupped the sides of his head in his hands. They said nothing.

"He's so small, Esther," he said after a moment. "Somehow I just never realized how very small he is.

Not till tonight. And I hit him. I actually *hit* him! My God, Esther, what kind of a brute am I to hit a . . . a *baby?*"

Esther rose and came to stand behind his chair, putting her hands on his shoulders. She leaned over and kissed the top of his head. "I know, Will, I know. Sometimes things happen. We shouldn't let them, but we do. I know you didn't mean it. Did you talk with him?"

He shook his head. "With him, no. To him. As always, *to* him. He just sat. Didn't talk, didn't move, wouldn't even look at me. I . . . told him I was sorry, but I just couldn't get through to him. Esther, believe me, I do love Ben — more, I think, than I ever realized — but I just can't seem to communicate with him. Is it me, Esther? Is there something the matter with me that I can't even talk with my own son?"

"He'll come around," Esther said softly. "You'll see. It just takes time, that's all. Time and understanding and a lot of patience; more patience, sometimes, than we think we can give. He'll come around, though."

"Sure he will, Dad," John interjected. "Don't you worry."

But the glance that John and his mother shared at that moment made it evident that neither was any longer quite so sure of it at all. They lapsed into silence and after a little while Esther spoke quietly.

"I'll go out and see to Ben now."

Chapter 6

For three days after returning to her burrow with the prairie dog, the female badger remained within the den, alternately nursing her pups, cleaning them and eating the remainder of her prey.

As all badgers are, she was fastidious about the condition of the den. Bones, feathers, bits of fur and other such residue were always buried well beneath the floor level of the emergency exit tunnel. And when the baby badgers defecated — neither often nor much — she would quickly consume their wastes and gently cleanse them with her tongue. She gave no indication of distaste for the chore and even appeared to gain a certain nutrient value from it. Without her ability to perform this act, the den would soon have become unbearably messy and would have reeked with the stench of such offal and body wastes.

Her own wastes she always contained within her until she was far from the den. Even then she would dig a hole in which to deposit them and then cover them over with dirt and debris. The only exception to this was when she was coming into her season, at which time she would leave the waste exposed so that the odor of it, mingled with musk from her scent glands, would attract a mate. A male badger could detect and follow up such a scent from as far distant as seven or eight miles.

But now, at the beginning of her fourth consecutive night in the den with her pups and with the prairie dog remains long since consumed, she felt the stirrings of hunger. She licked the three sightless babies thoroughly, and though they began squirming into position to nurse again, she nudged them away with her snout and left the den, wheezing softly.

As always, she paused at the entrance and emerged slowly, cautiously, listening and sniffing for possible danger. The breeze from the northeast was fresh and bore no sound or scent of hazard and so she came out all the way. There she stood upright on her hind legs and looked around carefully, especially toward the downwind direction from whence scent might not have reached her and sound might not have carried. Again there was no evidence of danger and without further delay she dropped to all fours and began her flowing gait toward the southwest.

She had traveled no more than a hundred feet when she stopped abruptly and her nose tilted upward, sniffing. There it was again, that same strange and compelling odor she had detected on her way back to the den with the prairie dog. Without hesitation now she turned to follow it and the scent trail led her more or less back toward the den. At about sixty feet from the entrance the smell was very heavy and she detected that it was coming from the ground directly in front of her. Camouflaged though it was, she could see that something had been buried here, something that smelled extremely enticing.

Still, her natural caution made her suspicious and she circled the area several times, ignoring the big slab of grass-cloaked rock nearby and concentrating her attention on the area of ground emanating the odor. Her circles grew smaller, her caution less, though her suspicions were not entirely allayed. At last she stopped with her nose directly over the spot. Whining with excitement stirred by the aroma, she reached her right front paw out gingerly and scratched the surface of the ground. It was loose and her claws pulled away the grassy debris scattered over the top. Again she reached out and sunk her claws in a little farther and drew her foreleg in. A dirt-covered, fleshy object, slender and two or three inches in length was pulled free. She smelled it, licked it hesitantly, then snatched it up in her mouth and wolfed it down. The heavy, oily taste excited her tremendously. It was fish, but of a kind she had never eaten before. With a somewhat less suspicious eagerness, she reached out with the same paw to expose some more.

The great claws dug in. She felt them touch more of the fish, but at the same time she detected a faint give to the ground, as if it was sinking ever so slightly under the weight of her paw.

Instantly, instinctively, she jerked back. Her reflexes

were incredibly swift, but not quite swift enough. Even as she recoiled, the steel jaws erupted from the ground. They snapped closed, catching not her whole paw well up onto the lower leg as was intended, but imprisoning the two outer toes of her right front foot. The bone in the outermost toe snapped at the impact, but the other did not. The jaws of the trap gripped these toes well in, almost to where they joined the paw, and the pain was excruciating for the badger.

Growling, shrieking, snarling, she lunged and thrashed and tore up the area, but the grip of those steel jaws was not to be broken. She bit at the trap itself, at the chain running from its end, at the heavy wire attaching it to the slab of rock, even at the rock itself, but all to no avail.

Thus began a period of incomparable agony and anguish. Time after time she fought the trap until exhaustion made her stop and lie panting and wheezing. She would rest then, constantly licking her paw, trying vainly to ease the throbbing pain in the now badly swollen toes. Both had enlarged to twice normal size, making it that much more unlikely that she would be able to pull herself free. Off and on throughout the night — and the day and the night that followed — she alternately struggled and rested. And by the dawning of the second morning all she had accomplished was to drag the slab of rock about forty feet closer to the entrance of the den than it had been in the beginning.

That was when the real anguish began, for now she could faintly hear the mewling cries of her hungry pups deep in the burrow. All young animals have great need to be fed regularly and often and the baby badgers were no exception. If the nourishing milk of the mother is denied them for long, they quickly weaken. Now they were at the very peak of their hunger and just as she could hear their cries, so too could they hear her struggles and whining, the growls and scuffling that accompanied her efforts to get free. And knowing it was her, the young ones cried all the more loudly and scrambled about in blind bewilderment in the den chamber, unable to understand why she did not come to them, unable yet to go themselves to her.

All through that day, too, she fought the trap, spurred on with a greater desperation by the voices of her young reaching her. Inch by painful inch she managed to move the heavy slab closer to the den until, by nightfall, she was no more than ten feet from the entrance. It was as close as she could come. The rock had now become so entangled with the long grasses that she could no longer budge it and, though her struggling persisted all through the third night, not another inch was gained.

Over twenty miles away, in a Winnipeg saloon, George Burton sat in a card game, trying to parlay his gains from the hide of the female badger's mate into a much tidier sum but thus far only barely holding his own. If he gave any thought to this trap in which the female badger was now weakening in her struggles, he gave no sign of it. As usual, he would check his trap line when he got around to it.

By sunup of the third morning of her imprisonment, the female badger could detect a change in the cries from her pups. They were uttered less frequently and were considerably weaker than they had been. By mid-afternoon she could hear them only at long intervals and by nightfall there was only quiet. During that fourth night in the trap she struggled hardly at all. Her own strength had badly failed and her tongue was thick from lack of water. In the morning, just after dawn, she heard one of her pups cry weakly, briefly. It seemed to trigger in her a last great burst of energy. She had been lying at this point on the back side of the rock slab, with it between her and her burrow. Now she lunged to her feet and raced for the hole with all her strength. The shock, when she came to the end of the slack in the chain and wire, was tremendous. It flipped her completely over and slammed her onto her back with such force that a huge wheezing expulsion of breath was forced from her. It did something else, too; it broke the bone of the second imprisoned toe. Now all that held the greatly distended digits in the trap was a little bit of muscle tissue, tendons and tautly stretched skin. And it was to this now, once she recovered, that she directed her attention.

She began to gnaw on her own flesh, nipping it away particle by particle, whining and grunting with her efforts. Still, the sun was at its zenith before the final strained white tendon parted and the female badger was free.

Ignoring the continuing pain in her foot, she hastened down the burrow to the den, whining loudly to let the pups know of her coming. There was no response. They were lying still on the den floor when she got there and when she touched her nose to the first, the little one was stiff and cold. The second, a little male, was warm and soft and he moved a little when she nudged him. The third, like the first, was dead.

She turned her full attention to the little male, licking him and chattering softly. She rolled over, exposing her badly swollen nipples to him, but the little one was so weak he could not even hold up his head for more than just a second or two. She moaned more and maneuvered so the nipple was pressing against his snout. Once or twice he tried to feed, but he was just too weak. He could not hold himself upright enough, could not grasp the nipple tightly enough, had not even the strength to suck. By nightfall, he too was dead.

The female badger nuzzled them for a while longer but after an hour or so she gave up. Moving to the emergency escape shaft, she tore at the tunneling until it collapsed and sealed itself and then, backing from the main entrance, she paused a foot or so from the den chamber and plugged this passageway in a similar manner. It was an instinctive maneuver, done mechanically with no real understanding on her part of why she did it. Not infrequently she had done the same thing even when abandoning a temporary den. Occasionally, especially in winter, she would plug an entrance while she was inside and thereby benefit from the added warmth and protection this afforded.

She headed due south after leaving the den, evidently intent upon traveling far away from this tragic place. The throbbing in her damaged foot, however, intensified with every mile covered until she was hobbling badly and no longer able even to touch the forepaw to the ground. And so, though she had covered less than five miles, she began to look for a place to hole up. Digging a temporary den was out of the question. There was no alternative except to seek out one of her old abandoned burrows and remain there until she had recovered her strength and her wound had healed.

She raised her head above the grasses and looked about her. There was a familiar jumble of protruding rocks a short distance ahead of her and a series of low, rolling knolls — one of them Hawk's Hill — vaguely in the moonlight to the east. The landmarks oriented her and now she struck off slightly to the southwest. Within another half-mile she found what she had been seeking: one of her own excavations of more than a year ago, close to another of the outcroppings of rock. It was a large hole, even larger than her den hole had been, though the tunneling here was not as extensive as that of the one she had just abandoned. The entry, fairly well hidden by grasses, was adjacent to a large, flat, somewhat basin-shaped rock upon which, during the time she had resided here, she had sometimes stretched out to bask in the sun. The hole angled down for over six feet before leveling off and continuing another eight feet to the chamber. This chamber was a great deal larger than the den chamber she had so recently dug. The fact that it was so big was not really of her doing. Whether by accident or design, she had tunneled directly toward the rock pile and into a hollow pocket in the earth that had evidently been formed in some bygone age by the upheaval of these rocks, two of which had touched ends and pushed upward against each other. The resultant hollow beneath them was cone-shaped, with a base diameter of about eight feet and a height to the peak of the cone of more than seven feet. Moonlight shone in dimly through several chinks at the top where the rocks met imperfectly, but there were no large holes.

Not more than two feet from where the entrance tunnel emerged into this hollow, the emergency tunnel left it. She followed this the twenty feet it ran before angling to the surface. Upon reaching the opening, she cautiously poked her head above ground. The moon was gone now, hidden behind a blanket of low, heavy clouds that had just moved in. The smell of a rainstorm coming was in the air and the grasses seemed to tremble and whisper among themselves in anticipation.

As with the front entry, the grasses here at the emergency exit had grown right to the very lip of the hole, perfectly camouflaging it. Rather than disturb them and mash them down by moving outside to turn around, she simply backed down the tunnel to the big chamber.

Satisfied that she would be safe here for the time being, she lay down and licked her injured foot briefly. It was difficult for her to do, since the injury was to the outer portion of the foot and she had to bend both neck and forepaw in order to reach it adequately. The pain this caused was too much and so she soon ceased her efforts.

Though she had slaked her severe thirst at a pothole en route to this den, hunger remained strong in her. Even more than satisfying this hunger, however, she needed to rest, to recuperate somewhat from her strenuous exertions of the past days and nights in the trap. She curled up to sleep, tucking her nose under her tail, her long fur tending to stand erect because of the way she was curled and making her look like some fuzzy, well-stuffed cushion.

She slept deeply, wheezing gently as she breathed. It seemed incredible that in so short a time she had lost her mate, lost her den, lost her pups and even lost a portion of her right front foot. She was still in considerable pain and her mammary glands were uncomfortably swollen with milk which would now remain undrunk. But she would survive. As is common in nature, the instinct for survival is amazingly strong.

Chapter 7

Benjamin MacDonald had absolutely no intention of running away. For one thing, even had he considered the notion he would have had no idea where to go. He had never been as far away as Winnipeg, only twenty miles away from the farm. His longest trips had been to church on Sundays in North Corners and even then only along the well-rutted wagon trail which led there. On his own he had never gone farther than the banks of the Red River less than a mile to the east — for which he had been scolded and made to promise he would not go there again by himself — or more than just a little over a mile in the prairies to north, west and south of the farm. This day, as it turned out, he went much farther, though inadvertently at the outset.

Dawn was slow in coming. Heavy clouds had rolled in sometime after midnight and far to the westward could be heard the muted rumblings of thunder. With John, Coral and Beth off for their last day of the school year and both his mother and father busy — William mending bridles in the barn, Esther kneading dough in the kitchen — Ben was left to amuse himself. It had never been a problem for him before and it was not now.

Since the evening when George Burton had brought the dead badger here there had been a sense of strain in the family. Ben could see that all of them — his father in particular — were making every effort to draw him out and to include him in every way possible in all they did. Even Beth had astonishingly stopped trying to give him orders and instead was acting overly solicitous.

For one who had been until now essentially ignored or at least simply taken too much for granted, the attention Ben was getting was a heady sort of experience for him. He was almost dazed by it and even though he was shrewd enough to realize that it was being done through conscious effort, it was nonetheless gratifying to him. The biggest change had been in his father. At every opportunity he was stopping to talk with Ben, ruffling his hair, squatting down to explain things to him, several times picking him up and carrying him around. The elder MacDonald seemed unable, as Ben had done, to stop brooding about how he had lashed out and struck the boy. Twice more since that first night in the barn, he had apologized.

And Ben, for his part, was opening up a little. He did not attach nearly as much importance to his father's striking him as William MacDonald himself obviously did. In his own mind, Ben realized that he had been guilty of a deep transgression: he had actually run up and in fury struck his own father. And as much as his father wished forgiveness, so too did Ben, but unlike his father he was unprepared to express it in words. Therefore, the next best thing was to show it in actions, so he smiled more and paid more attention to what was being said. He answered — albeit as shortly as possible — when spoken to and clearly enjoyed the attention being lavished upon him of late.

With all these improvements, there was no reason in the world why Ben should have run away. As a matter of fact, he didn't; but he did *wander* away. Not very long after breakfast he watched Beth, Coral and John ride off, all fresh and clean in their Sunday best for this final day of school, John on his own horse, Beth and Coral doubled up on another. They had all turned and waved to him and shouted " 'Bye, Ben!" and he had waved back. After they were gone he played for a while on the mound of fresh earth beside the new well his father and John had been digging. But observation was more to Ben's preference than games of make-believe and so he left the pile and walked along the corral fence to its corner, perhaps fifty yards south of the house. It was here that he flushed the big prairie chicken.

The bird leaped up from the grasses close to the corner post and went thrashing off down the slope of Hawk's Hill, trailing a wing and clucking in an agitated manner. Ben knew at once there must be a nest nearby and he determined to look for it later, but for the moment his full concentration was on the bird. Holding his right hand to his right armpit and letting his left arm trail limply, he crouched and began following the bird, clucking as it clucked and emulating every action it made, even to the bobbing of its head.

The bird continued to move along, keeping ahead of him by about a dozen feet, clucking and thrashing about less frequently now that they were away from the immediate nest area, but still leading him directly away from it. To the bottom of Hawk's Hill they went and up the next rise. By now the prairie chicken hen was no longer trailing her wing and rarely making any vocal sound. Once or twice she made short hopping flights of a dozen yards or so forward, at which time Ben would run after her flapping his arms and leaping as if he truly believed that on one of those leaps he would leave the ground and fly as the bird ahead was doing.

And then, midway down the second slope, she took off with a powerful drumming of her wings and, flying low to the grasses, disappeared over the rim of yet another hill ahead. Ben raced after her, making a thrumming sound with his mouth to emulate that which had been given off by her wingbeats. He ran until he was to the point where she disappeared, even though he knew she would no longer be there. He was panting heavily when he stopped.

"Go on, you bird!" he shouted into the air, then grinned at himself. As rarely as he spoke to other people, he even less often spoke aloud to himself and as if it were a new power he had just discovered, he cupped his mouth and shouted again.

"Go on, you big old bird! Go on back to your nest and eggs. You didn't fool me."

The prairie swallowed up his words and they were further nullified by a dull rumble of thunder. He looked at the sky. It seemed no more leaden than it had been all morning and he was not yet ready to turn around and go home, so he walked on. He climbed and descended several more slopes and then, off in the distance, he saw a peregrine falcon winging swiftly along and watched it. The bird circled once over a marsh-fringed pothole and then went on. Ben grunted, wishing the bird had come closer. When it was gone, he headed for the pond himself. He had not been to this one before.

The bank was too heavily reed-choked for him to get close to the water, but through a little gap in the stems he did manage to see a painted turtle briefly stick its head above the surface near the middle, then submerge again. A belted kingfisher appeared from nowhere, hovered over the water, and then plunged into it, reappearing a moment later with its beak empty. It trilled its rattling cry as if in disgust over its own poor aim and then bounced off through the air on inconstant wingbeats.

Again Ben moved on. At one point, on the second slope from the pothole, he paused to watch a brilliant little goldfinch balanced on a stem, swaying up and down on this impromptu springboard in the freshening breeze, its black wings folded neatly alongside the butter yellow of its body plumage and a little black patch on its forehead to match the wings and tail. At another point, farther on, he ran and jumped along, trying to keep up with a butterfly in its erratic, weightless flight over the grasses. Suddenly its little form whirled away before a gust of wind heavier than any of the others up to now.

Again Ben looked at the sky and he frowned. It was much darker now than it had been and he wondered why he hadn't noticed before this how much nearer the thunder sounded. It was probably past lunchtime already and definitely time to be starting home.

He began to walk swiftly in the direction he felt was right, guilty about having gone so far from home. But an hour later he was still walking, though not swiftly and with a niggling uncertainty sprouting in his mind. The day had been sunless and still was, and he realized with a shock that he couldn't even be certain of the direction in which he was moving. The fields looked the same everywhere and so did the rolling hills. There was no trace of the familiar buildings which perched on the crest of Hawk's Hill. There were potholes here and there in the distance, but none of them looked like any with which he was familiar, and the same held true for the isolated rock outcroppings.

Another hour passed, then two. It was certainly well past midafternoon now but still nothing looked at all familiar to him and he had the momentary panicky feeling that somehow, like the little girl in the story his mother had read to him, he had stepped into another world. The swirling, menacing clouds seemed to be closing in on him, the wind tearing at his shirt and trousers and hair. A rock pile loomed a quarter-mile ahead and he began running down the slope toward it in an effort to reach it before the rains came. He fell, scrambled up with one of his shoes gone, and plunged on. His other shoe flew off a few moments later but he didn't stop. He reached the rocks just as the first pelting drops began falling and by this time he was hobbling, as the soles of both stockinged feet were hurting from contact with the ground.

The outcropping of rocks was disappointingly smaller than it had seemed from the distance and there was no cover in it, no hollow in which to crouch to wait out the rain with reasonable shelter. He was afraid now, blinded as much by his own tears as by the stinging rain which struck his face. Only a short distance away the prairie had all but disappeared in the torrential downpour sweeping his way, and not knowing what else to do, he turned and ran away from it as if believing he would be able to outrun it.

Suddenly his foot came down and there was no ground where there should have been. A small scream escaped him as he sprawled full length in the wet grass and he sat up quickly, hugging one leg and crying harder now. His pants had torn and his knee was scraped and oozing blood from contact with a rock.

He looked for what had tripped him and saw, beside the rock, a large hole.

The rain was upon him at that same moment in its fullest fury, drenching him in an instant, washing away whatever hope he had of escaping it. Hardly thinking, he thrust his legs, feet close together, into the hole and shoved himself backwards and downwards into it. His slightness was in his favor, but even so it was a snug fit as he inched his way in. At shoulder depth the narrowness of the entry stopped him and he pulled himself out a little and then reached back, clawing with his fingers to enlarge the opening. His sobs were lost in the slashing of the rain.

The barehanded digging was raising his fingernails and they hurt, but still he kept on digging. At last he was able to back in farther and found that inside a short distance the burrow was a bit roomier. Though his shoulders still brushed the tunnel sides and he had to keep his arms outstretched over his head, he was no longer so compressed by the walls. He continued backing until the rain was no longer hitting his head and arms. Then, with mingled tears and rainwater dribbling from his chin, he stopped and simply lay there while the rivulets of rain running down the slope of the hole saturated his stomach.

The rain continued throughout the remainder of the daylight hours. Occasionally it would slacken considerably but just as he would be on the point of emerging, the skies would open with another deluge. If he had known the way home he would have come out in spite of the storm and headed that way, but he just had no idea which way to go. He had never before felt so small, so all alone, so afraid.

The grayness of the day deepened with the approach of night and the ground still vibrated frighteningly in sympathy with the thunder. A searing bolt of lightning cracked with such fantastic force close at hand that he wet his pants with fear. The acrid smell of ozone was in the air and he buried his face in the dirt of the tunnel floor as a new spasm of sobs shook him. But that close strike of the lightning seemed to be something of a finale for a while. The rain eased off until it was little more than a heavy drizzle, though in the distance the thunder continued rumbling almost constantly.

It had been dark for the better part of an hour and Ben was in a state of semi-sleep when his head suddenly jerked up. From outside he could hear a strange sound approaching, an intermingled wheezing and grumbling. Not much light was coming into the burrow from outside but there was enough difference in the darkness that when the vague illumination of the entry was suddenly blocked out by the deep, solid bulk of something entering, he knew it. He was vulnerable in the extreme and terrified, not able in these initial moments to even imagine what this thing might be.

The large female badger, still greatly favoring her injured forepaw, had been away from the burrow since the forenoon. Hunger had driven her to hunt and since the nature of her injury prevented her from digging for her prey, she had gone from pothole to pothole, catching green frogs and leopard frogs and even the runt of a newly hatched brood of mallard ducklings. Even through the rain she had continued hunting and finally, with hunger appeased to some degree, she had returned to the rock-pile burrow to rest again. It was not until she was partially inside that she sensed the boy and instantly she snarled viciously. In such confines it was a horrifying sound.

"Get out! *Get out!*" Ben screamed. His extended hand clenched the muddy earth and he tried to pitch a handful at her, though without much success.

The throaty, snarling growls increased, and instead of retreating, the badger came even deeper into the hole. They were now uncomfortably close together and Ben shouted at her again to get away. Her head was nearly to his hand and he shoved forward a little and tried to scratch at her eyes and now he, too, snarled; not as menacingly as she, perhaps, but with nonetheless remarkable mimicry of the sound she was making.

As he lashed at her with his hand, so she lashed back at him with her forepaw, forgetting for the moment its injury. Two of the three remaining claws on her paw barely touched his cheek and scratched it. His was the greater fear, but hers the greater pain. She whined sharply and withdrew the paw, backing up slightly.

The rain had recommenced and was now drumming down steadily. The position the badger was in was uncomfortable and her rear quarters were getting drenched. Her snarling died and she uttered a low chattering sound different from any Ben had heard before, yet close enough to that which he remembered that he now realized that this was a badger before him.

No longer crying now and gaining a little assurance with the backing-off of the animal, Ben chattered back at her, not only the way she had just now chattered, but also with the chatter he had learned at their prairie encounter. He could not believe this would be the same badger, since he was so far away from where he saw that one, but he hoped the sound would keep this animal from pressing an attack. He chattered again and was relieved to see her back out of the burrow entirely. A waft of fresh moist air came in, followed by a new trickle of water running down the tunnel.

Though Ben watched up the burrow toward its mouth for a long time, the bulky shadow did not re-appear. The badger had gone. And at last, wet, cold, cramped, and dreadfully weary, Benjamin MacDonald slept.

Chapter 8

It had been a bad night for Ben. Exhausted though he was, he slept only fitfully at best in the badger hole. One time he had awakened thinking he had heard someone call his name, but though he listened intently, all he heard after that was the persistent slashing of the rain and booming of thunder. And time after time as the night progressed he had awakened with a start from his dozing and stared up the burrow, expecting every time to see the bulky shadow of the badger blocking the entry. And once more it had.

About the middle of the night she had come again, thrusting head and forelegs into the hole until she was no more than a foot from the boy. It was her soft wheezing accompanied by a peculiar whining which roused him. This time, however, Ben was nowhere near as afraid as he had been at first. Rather, he was angry and he scolded the animal sharply.

"Why don't you go away and leave me alone!" he said loudly. "What do you want, anyway? If this is your hole, it's just too bad. I'm using it now. You just go on away, you hear me? Get out of here!"

The badger merely cocked her head and let a faint hiss escape her. Even when Ben scooped up another handful of muddy dirt and tossed it at her, she did no more than flinch and growl a little. Ben promptly growled back at her and then chattered in the various ways he had heard her chatter. For an instant it had seemed she would come in even more, but then she backed out and was gone again.

Rain was still falling rather steadily but the thunder and lightning had ended. In a moment the trickle of water resumed running down the hole and Ben bent his head and tried to lap some up with his tongue. It was so heavy with mud, however, that it nearly made him gag and so he stopped and bent one arm back far enough that he could rest his head on it. After a while he fell asleep once more. As the night wore on he cried out several times in his sleep for his mother and he moaned frequently. Once he woke himself up shouting, "Get out of here!" but the badger was not there.

Just before dawn he fell into a much deeper sleep and it was not until an hour or more after sunrise that he woke again. The rain had stopped and in the oval view of the sky that was visible to him he could see bright blue and occasionally little white puffs of clouds drifting past.

He groaned when first he moved, his body stiff and aching from being so long in one position. He looked at his hands and they were so caked with mud that he could not see the skin and from the way his face felt, he knew it must be in the same condition. Remembrance of the events of the night came to him and he shuddered. Had it all been a dream? Had he just imagined that a badger had come and tried to get down this hole? It had seemed so real, and yet there was no sign of the animal now.

It dawned on him that he was terribly hungry as well as being thirsty. His mouth was gritty and had a muddy taste. He spat several times against the side of the tunnel to rid himself of it, but could not. After a few minutes he began to inch his way up the tunnel. The fact that he had lost his shoes was now a help to him, because he could draw his legs up a little and dig his toes into the earth where the floor of the tunnel met the sides. Thrusting in this way with his feet and likewise digging his fingers in ahead of him, he slowly squirmed his way back to the surface.

The brightness of the morning sun made him squint as he raised his head and shoulders above the hole. The broad, basin-shaped slab of rock beside the entrance had filled with water — a gallon or more of it — and it was clear and inviting under the slanting rays of the sun. He dipped his head to it and drank greedily, sucking the water in with an extravagant slurping and gulping. He raised his head, gasping, belched out some of the air he had swallowed, and drank again. The water was muddying where his face touched it and he looked at his hands again and wrinkled his nose at their condition.

He was on the point of washing them clean in the puddle when he hesitated. No, he might want another drink before he left here. He was distinctly proud of such foresight. He came out of the hole the rest of the way and again frowned as he saw the condition of his clothes: shoes gone, socks nearly pulled off, trousers torn, everything he wore saturated by water and heavy with mud. His scraped knee beneath the rip in his trousers was caked with mud and he touched it gingerly, wincing a little.

He pulled his socks the rest of the way off, squeezed what water he could out of them, and put them in his pants pocket. Droplets of water glistened diamond-like with reflected sunlight on the surrounding grasses and he got up stiffly and walked into the heaviest nearby growth. Almost immediately his pants from the knees down became newly saturated and his bare feet, sliding against the grass, were being cleansed of mud. He ran a little way and stopped. Almost all the mud was gone from his feet and the trouser legs were extremely wet, but nowhere near as muddy as they had been. He dropped to hands and knees and swung his arms back and forth through the grasses, advancing a little with each swing. He was delighted with how the mud was being washed away. When his hands were clean he got them good and wet in the same manner and then scrubbed at his face, feeling the mud there become slick and then begin coming away on his hands. The job he did was far from thorough. When he gave up he had cleaned a circle of his face which took in the eyes, nose and mouth, but leaving a fairly heavy border of muddiness all around, so that he looked ludicrously like a monkey with a bare face framed in dark fur.

The flapping of his torn trouser leg bothered him, so he ripped it off at the knee. It felt better and he tried to rip the other one off the same way, but he was not strong enough to get the initial tear started, so he finally gave up the attempt. His hair was heavily plastered with mud, but except for running his hands through it several times to get rid of the biggest lumps, there was little he could do with it.

He was thirsty again and suddenly very glad indeed that he had not badly muddied up the water which had collected in the depression of the flat rock. He returned to it and drank again, less noisily this time. He sat on the ground beside rock and hole and for the first time this morning considered his predicament. He still had no idea whatever where he was. The rolling fields looked bewilderingly the same in all directions and the scattered potholes and rocky outcroppings he could see appeared virtually identical to him. He tried to remember from which direction he had arrived at this point but his running and stumbling to escape the rain, along with the hours of confused wandering before that, had completely disoriented him.

He thought of the badger again and very nearly concluded that the night's encounters had simply been a dream. Yet it had seemed so real! Even now he could remember the sounds the fierce animal had made — the ferocious snarls and hissings and deep growls, the whinings and the gruntings. Could he have dreamed all that? And if it really wasn't a dream, then where was the badger now? Why was there no sign of it? His gaze swept around the vicinity and then paused at the hole near his feet. There *was* a sign! With a little exclamation he got to hands and knees and looked at the marks in the mud where his own hands or feet or knees had made contact, but what was this . . . and this . . . and *this*? They were the tracks of an animal, a big animal. The footprints were easily three and a half inches long and correspondingly broad. Toe prints were there as well and, at the ends of these, the deeper gouges made by claws. It hadn't been a dream after all; a badger had come here last night, probably even early this morning as he slept, or the tracks would have been obliterated by the rain.

Again he looked around, more carefully now, but except for a little flock of red-winged blackbirds in ragged flight disappearing over the closest hill, there was nothing moving that he could see. The low rock pile to his right blocked his view in that direction and he moved over that way to see what was behind it. At the base of the rocks some wild roses were growing and he suddenly stopped and plucked four or five of the plump rose hips that had formed. He popped one of these into his mouth and chewed, made a wry face and was on the point of spitting it out, but then hunger prevailed and he continued chewing and swallowed it. One by one he ate the others, though his distaste was evident. He looked around for more, found two others he had missed and ate them also. They did little to satisfy his hunger, but at least his stomach had something to work on.

From a distance beyond the rock pile he heard a noise he couldn't identify and a natural caution took hold of him. Carefully he moved and peeked around the rocks and for an instant felt a surge of excitement as he saw a man riding a horse no more than a quarter-mile distant to the west. He couldn't tell who it was and he was considering running out with wildly waving arms to attract the rider's attention when he saw the dog. It was a big, yellowish-gray mongrel and there was no doubt to whom it belonged. It was Lobo, George Burton's dog. Studying the rider himself more closely now, Ben could just make out the heavy darkness of the man's face which was not shadow but rather the big man's dense black beard.

Almost without thinking, Ben backed out of sight. His hatred for this trapper was such that he was actually trembling. The man was angling right toward this area and Ben, with fear and distrust heavy within him, scrambled on hands and feet back to the burrow and slid himself backwards deep into the shelter of it.

He waited a long time without hearing a sound. He concluded that Burton must surely have gone off in another direction. Slowly, carefully, he raised his head from the hole. The grasses blocked his view and he put his palms flat to the ground on either side of the opening and lifted himself even higher. He sucked in his breath. Burton had stopped his horse no more than fifty yards away. His left side was toward Ben and he was shading his eyes with one hand as he scanned the green hills to the eastward. Lobo stood alertly with his muzzle raised and his head turned slightly toward Ben, as if for just an instant a vagrant breeze had brought him the boy's scent, but then he relaxed and merely stood patiently as he waited for his master to move on.

Ben ducked back into the hole, shoving himself downward until it became too narrow for him to go any farther. There he lay with the pulsing of his own heart so loud in his ears that he thought sure the trapper or his dog must hear it. For fully fifteen minutes he remained where he was and only then did he slowly inch his way back to the surface to take another look.

A sigh of relief escaped him. Burton was now far away toward the southeast, the dog beyond sight and the bottom half of the horse already hidden by the crest of a hill. Keeping well down, Ben watched until the rider was gradually swallowed up.

Any thought Ben had harbored of trying to find his way home over the prairies was now discarded. He was sure that as soon as he exposed himself Burton would catch him. Just exactly what the trapper might do to him he didn't try to imagine, but he was terribly afraid of the man and very determined that Burton should not see him.

More grateful than ever for the puddle on the rock, Ben drank from it again and stretched out on his back at full length on the ground. The sun was warm and felt good on his body. The exhaustion he had experienced and the restless night had taken their toll and now he grew very sleepy. He dozed for a few minutes, dreamed that Burton had ridden up and was sitting on his horse staring down at him with his lips split in a wide, evil grin and the yellowed teeth framed by the bushy beard. He awoke with a start, trembling, and immediately backed down the hole again until his head was a foot or more below ground level. In a short while the sleepiness returned and he shut his eyes. This time his slumber was deep and dreamless.

He slept for four hours and when he awakened, the female badger was there. She was, in fact, already starting to descend into the burrow with a partially devoured prairie chicken in her mouth. Ben yelled at her and she stopped, opening her mouth to snarl at him and dropping the bird in the process. It rolled over once toward him and he snatched at it and caught it by a leg and pulled it to himself.

The snarling of the badger died away and was replaced by a low, curious whining. Ben made the same sound, watching the animal closely. Strangely, now that it was daylight he no longer felt so afraid of the creature. He looked curiously at that broad, white-streaked head, at the intelligent eyes studying him so close to his own face and he saw no sign of fear there, no indication of intent to attack. There was only a sort of returned curiosity about this diminutive human being in the burrow.

Ben, with this opportunity for closer examination of

the animal by daylight, noted two things specifically about her. One was the deeply notched right ear and he smiled when he saw it.

"You're the same one," he said softly. "You're the one I fed the baby mice to, aren't you?"

The badger snarled again faintly at the sound of his voice and a low hiss issued from her mouth, but then she cocked her head as if intrigued by the strange sounds he was making. She moved inward just a little more and it was then that Ben noticed the second thing. Her right front foot was grossly swollen and the two outermost toes were newly missing. He frowned and made a little sympathetic sound.

"You hurt your foot, badger," he said. "I bet it really hurt. I wonder how it happened?"

The big female badger cocked her head again and a steady chattering noise left her. Ben grinned and mimicked the sound and then grinned even more broadly when she cocked her head the other way. He moved his hand forward to touch her but she jerked back, though she still stayed in the burrow entrance.

Except for the handful of rose hips he had eaten earlier this morning, Ben had had no food since breakfast the day before and he was ravenous. He looked at the remains of the bird the badger had dropped. The head and neck were eaten away and most of the viscera had been devoured as well as a small portion of one side. It looked far from appetizing but Ben was too hungry to care. He tried to break off a leg but it only twisted in his grip and he could not even snap the bone. He made an exasperated sound and ripped away the skin and feathers of the plump breast and brought the meat to his mouth. The first bite he took was small, tentative, hard to pull free. He wound up with only a little chunk of the flesh but he chewed it up and was surprised at the good taste of it, despite the fact that it was raw. He attacked the bird more eagerly then, grinding his teeth through the tissues and yanking out bigger bites. The more of it he ate, the more it appealed to him and he concentrated his whole attention on it. It was only when he suddenly became aware that it was considerably lighter in the burrow — and had been for some time — that he realized the badger had gone away again.

He continued eating and had consumed much of one side of the breast and had started gnawing on a thigh when he had a momentary start. Deep inside the hole something soft and moist had touched his bare foot. His eyes widened and for just an instant the fear gripped him again. It happened a second time, but now it was more prolonged and along with the soft, warm wetness, he felt a furriness as well. The badger! Evidently the animal had come in from another tunnel and was now behind him, licking his bare foot.

He suddenly giggled. It tickled. He wiggled his feet and snickered again. "Stop it," he said. "Quit doing that, badger!"

The licking continued and he laughed aloud, unable to stand it. He dug fingers and toes into the earth and began pulling himself upward and out, clenching what remained of the bird in his teeth. Remembering Burton, he paused and looked around with great care before fully exposing himself and even then he did not stand up. He drank again from the puddle and sat cross-legged on the ground, watching the burrow and expecting to see the badger emerge from it. She did not and after a little while he began gnawing at the bird again.

He finished eating the flesh from the bones of thigh and leg and when he next looked around, the badger was crouched quietly six or seven feet away from him in the grass, watching him eat. She had not emerged from this hole here and so, Ben reasoned, she must have come out of the other exit. Once more he tried to break off a piece of the bird to give it to her, but the tendons were too tough and he could not. Inside the body cavity, however, the heart and lungs were still in place, along with a portion of the liver. He scooped these out with one hand and held them toward the badger.

She showed her teeth briefly as if to snarl and then simply looked at him. When it became obvious that she would not come any closer, he shrugged and pitched the organs toward her. She stretched her neck and sniffed at them where they had fallen just in front of her. With cautious daintiness then, she turned her head slightly to one side and picked them up in her teeth, tossed them back into her mouth and ate them.

"You're hungry, too," Ben said, smiling. "Sure glad you brought this bird. I was awful hungry. Want more?"

He tried a third time to break off a piece with his hands and when he could not, he tried biting a limb off, but still without success. A flat, ragged-edged fragment of rock lay half hidden in the grass close to the puddle rock and he worked it back and forth until the end that was buried in the ground came loose and he pulled it free. With this primitive tool he began sawing at the other leg of the bird close to the body. When that didn't work well, he put the remains on the edge of the puddle rock and held it with one hand while he pounded at it with the sharp stone in the other. Momentarily the badger grew nervous but as the boy continued to work at it without even looking at her, she relaxed. Gradually the fibers of meat and tendon were parting and after a few minutes he managed to free a shapeless mass. This, too, he tossed to her.

The badger picked it up and then lay down with it under her front forepaw. Instead of wolfing it down as a dog might have done, she held it in this way as she gnawed slowly at it like a cat, chewing off small pieces and swallowing them.

Ben, too, continued eating. By the time the badger finished eating this latest piece he had given her, the boy had had enough of the bird. He was satisfied with what he had eaten and he tossed what was left to her, then immediately regretted doing so when he realized that he would be hungry again later on and he should have saved it for then. He thought of perhaps taking it back from her but decided against it. Instead, he drank again from the puddle and turned his attention to the burrow. He picked up the rock chip again and now he got down on his stomach and crawled head-first into the hole. Using the rock as a gouging tool, he began enlarging the hole; not so much near the entry and a few feet in, where he could already slide his thin form through, but a good bit deeper inside.

The dirt he dislodged piled up on the tunnel floor in front of him and when it became a mound which hampered him, he backed out of the hole, still gripping the rock in one hand and a handful of fresh dirt in the other. He looked at it and shook his head. It was a pitifully small amount. At this rate he would be all day just bringing to the surface what he had already dug.

He looked around for the badger but again she was gone, and for the first time he felt a pang of loneliness at her having left him. Nevertheless, he felt reasonably sure she'd be back and he returned his attention to the problem of the dirt. He had no intention of digging in very much farther, but he did want to hollow out a cavity down there large enough for him to cuddle in without being so cramped, and also large enough so that he could enter the burrow headfirst and turn around when he got down there. That there might already be a chamber somewhere down there did not occur to him; he thought of it only as a long tunnel with an entrance and an exit. But the problem still

remained of removing the earth he would dislodge.

An idea occurred to him and he laughed aloud softly at his own cleverness. He untied the rawhide cord which he used as a belt and pulled off his trousers. Then he bunched the waist of the trousers together quite firmly, pulled the cord snug and tied it in a triple knot. By carrying it into the hole with him and stuffing dirt into the leg, he would be able to bring out quite a quantity each time. He might lose some, he supposed, through the leg torn off at the knee and so he took one of his socks from his pocket and tied it tightly around the trouser leg at the crotch. He laughed again, proud of his own ingenuity and achievement, and reentered the burrow. He had to push a hole through the accumulated dirt to get the trousers through it and then, with the tied waist of the pants farther down the hole and the open leg toward him, he began stuffing dirt into it. The makeshift container held much more than he had thought it would, taking not only all that he had already dislodged, but even some that he now hollowed out to fill it up.

He backed to the surface with his first load and scattered it in the grass. Suddenly he ducked until only his head from the eyes up was showing above the buffalo grass. Far in the distance a horseman was riding, changing direction frequently but angling generally southwestward. Though there was no sign of the dog Lobo, Ben was sure the rider had to be Burton again. He continued to watch closely, prepared to duck down the hole, but except for turning in this direction briefly once or twice, the horseman never approached nearer than about five hundred yards. When at last he disappeared over a rise far to the southwest, where once again dark clouds were building on the horizon, Ben returned to the burrow and resumed his work.

He was about to the point where he planned to make a larger cavity when he detected that the tunnel was changing. It was no longer angling downward but instead moving off parallel with ground level. He stuck his head far down to stare into the darkness and then sucked in his breath. Instead of an absolute blackness as he more or less anticipated, the tunnel was just vaguely visible stretching ahead of him, and another eight feet farther on, it expanded into some sort of a dimly visible chamber.

All thought of digging a hollow of his own left him now and he worked with renewed energy, heading toward that opening ahead. Five times he backed to the surface to empty the bulging trousers, scattering the dirt by swinging the trousers around in a circle rather than just dumping it in a pile. On the fifth emptying he spied another horseman, much closer. He could see it wasn't Burton, but equally he could see that it was no one he could recognize. Immediately he scrambled on hands and knees through the grass back to the burrow and plunged in headfirst. He went down to the turn and lay there quietly for half an hour, but heard no sound in all that time. Again he moved forward and this time, with the trouser-bag only half full, he was able to get into the chamber.

Pushing the trousers ahead of him, he drew himself into the room, tossed the load of dirt still in the pants to one side and was delighted to find that he could actually stand up. Though illumination through the chinks and cracks in the rocks above was faint at best, his eyes were by this time so accustomed to the darkness of the tunnel that the interior of the room was quite plainly visible to him.

He inspected the large conical chamber thoroughly, feeling the dried grasses and clumps of browned, long-dead moss, bending over with his face nearly at floor level to peer into the impenetrable darkness of the long escape tunnel so close to the one he had entered by.

It was a combination of thirst and curiosity which, after a bit, sent him squirming — headfirst this time — back to the surface. Far, far in the distance directly south was a speck which had to be a horseman, but whether or not it was the last one he had seen or yet another, Ben could not determine. There was no danger at such distance that he himself would be seen and so he drank his fill from the now considerably diminished rock puddle.

A gnawing loneliness was gripping him again, now that he had nothing to occupy his attention, and unexpectedly he felt tears welling in his eyes.

"Mama," he said aloud, though softly. "Mama, where are you?"

The only answer was a swishing and rustling of the grasses in a freshening breeze and the first dull rollings of thunder in the western distance. With his bare legs exposed to the breeze, he suddenly trembled. He was getting hungry again and he wished he had not given the remains of the prairie chicken to the badger. He went to the spot where she had taken it but nothing was there, not even a bone.

And then he was crying, with great shuddering sobs wracking his little body, standing there alone and dwarfed by the immensity of the prairie around him and the limitless sky above. He sat by the entrance of the den and every now and then, interspersed with his sobbing, he would call for his mother. Several times he said the name of his big brother, John, and once in a plaintive and subdued way he even called, "Daddy!"

Chapter 9

On the day of Ben's disappearance, Esther MacDonald had experienced no real sense of concern until about noon. She had looked outside several times and, not seeing her son, had dared to hope that Ben was with his father and that William was nurturing the faint degree of communication that seemed to be developing between them. Twice as the morning progressed she nearly went out to the barn to check, but each time she stopped herself from doing so. If there was in fact some sort of rapport developing between father and son, she wanted to do nothing that might interrupt.

Only when, shortly after noon at her ringing of the metal triangle on the porch, William came in without Ben did her worry become focused. William MacDonald, for his part, admitted that he too had looked out a time or two as he worked in the barn and, not seeing his little son playing outside, figured he must be in the house with his mother.

Esther stepped out on the porch, rang the heavy triangle again and then, not satisfied, cupped her mouth and called.

"Bennnnn. Benjaminnnnn."

No answer. The only sound she could hear was that of the muted, far-distant thunder. She frowned and bit her lower lip. That wasn't like Ben at all. She came back into the kitchen where William was seated at the table, eating. When he looked up at her she shook her head and her brow wrinkled faintly.

"He doesn't answer. Now where do you suppose that boy could have gotten to?"

MacDonald did not appear perturbed. "Knowing Ben," he said, cutting a slab of fresh bread from the loaf Esther had baked, "he's probably out talking with a chipmunk." He grinned to show he was just joking, but Esther bridled.

"That's not funny, William. Ben's your own son."

MacDonald shrugged. "Guess it wasn't funny at that," he admitted, "but I wasn't ridiculing him. I wouldn't worry about him, honey. The point I was trying to make was, you know how he's sometimes out for hours watching a wasp build its nest or following one of the sheep or any number of things. He probably just let the time slip away on him and he'll be running home any minute now. Fact is, he probably heard you clanging for lunch wherever he is and I expect he's on his way now. Sit down and eat. If he's not back when we're finished, I'll go scout him up."

Esther was mollified. "Well, all right," she said, sitting down at her place, "but Will, please don't yell at him for missing lunch. Time means nothing to little ones like that. Just bring him home and let me be the

134

one to explain to him that he should try to remember to be here when lunch is ready."

But when the meal was finished and Ben still had not shown up, Esther's worry returned and magnified. She went outside with William and they separated, checking in the barn, loft, outbuildings, cattle and sheep sheds, everywhere, their calls for him ringing in the air at frequent intervals. They came together again near the front porch and now the contagion of Esther's worry had spread to Ben's father.

"Can't understand it," he said slowly. "Where do you suppose he got to?"

"I don't know, Will. I just don't know. But I'm getting scared now. You don't think he could have gotten hurt somewhere, do you?"

MacDonald shook his head. "Hard saying, though I suppose he might've. Let's think back to where we last saw him. I think I saw him last over there, playing on the dirt pile by the —" He stopped and swallowed.

Esther's eyes widened. "Oh God, did he fall into the new well?"

They ran over to the spot together and looked fearfully into the big hole. The excavation was already about eighteen feet deep and MacDonald had anticipated hitting water within another three or four feet. But the bottom was empty. Esther leaned against William's chest and cupped her forehead in one hand. Reaction had made her half sick; relief that the child had not tumbled into the hole, yet increased worry because he still was not found. MacDonald patted her clumsily for a moment and then pointed at the dirt pile.

"His tracks are there in the new dirt, but no way of telling from them which way he went from here. I'll get Dover saddled and take a little ride. Maybe he strayed off farther than he intended."

Esther touched his arm and then tilted her head toward the heavy clouds building up in the west. "Find him soon, Will."

He nodded grimly. "I'll find him. Don't worry."

But William MacDonald didn't find Ben. For over an hour he ranged in ever-widening circles around the house on Hawk's Hill, pausing here and there to stand high in the stirrups and shout Ben's name while continuing to scan the sea of grass for even the faintest sign of him. More and more he swung his gaze toward the tree-flanked Red River almost a mile from the house. Time and again Ben had been warned against going down there near the swift river to play and he had promised that he wouldn't. But maybe, just maybe, this time he had.

He struck out on a zigzagging course in that direction, but again there was no sign of Ben there or along the way. A chilling fear was gripping him now. The very helplessness of the boy, his small size, his total defenselessness, all were added weights in his mind and he began imagining things: there had been no trouble with wolves in recent years, but might one have attacked him? A badger, too, could be very dangerous, and Ben had only recently seen one. And what about the bears? The big lumbering black bears were normally shy and inoffensive, but suppose Ben had inadvertently blundered into one, surprising him? Might not the animal have attacked? What about the wolverines that sometimes moved down this way? They were mean ones, those animals, and even though it was usually winter before any showed up around here, suppose one did and encountered Ben? The pictures MacDonald was painting in his own mind sickened him and he shook himself as if to throw them off. He renewed his searching.

Close to four in the afternoon, with the storm almost upon him, he came back to the house mentally praying that he would find Ben had returned. Esther was on the porch and clustered around her were John, Beth, and Coral, just returned from school. One glance at the anxiety in each expression was enough to show that Ben had not come home. He shook his head and Esther stifled a cry. MacDonald directed his gaze at his eldest son.

"John, get your slicker on. Range out toward the north and northwest for any sign of him. Stay within a couple of miles of the house. I can't imagine Ben going any farther away than that. I've already checked between here and the river and a little to the south along the bank. Nothing. You keep on looking till I get back. Beth, you and Coral help your mother. Look everywhere around here — *everywhere!* — in the attic, storm cellar, under beds, in the barn, wherever. We've checked all around, but look again. Pay attention to small places; any sort of place that he might have squeezed himself into.

"Esther, honey," he added, "I'm going for help. I'll get Burton, McKinzie, Scortie, and some of the others nearby to help search and I'll send someone off to North Corners to raise a bigger search party. No time to waste now. Be back as soon as possible."

He reined Dover around and dug his heels into the big gelding's flanks. The black horse galloped off down the wagon trail toward the southeast. It was just about then that the downpour began.

The men came; Burton first, since his place was closest, then others by themselves or in groups of two or three or four. William MacDonald himself returned with all four of the gangling Billington boys, telling Esther hurriedly that Joe Billington had sent his sons along and had himself volunteered to ride on to North Corners to organize a search party.

The men and boys spread out in all directions, squinting against the pelting rain, their calls for Ben drowned out by thunder and drumming rain or whipped away by the gusting wind. Just before dark three wagons and four buggies, escorted by eleven mounted men, reached the house on Hawk's Hill. Some of the womenfolk had come along to stay at the house with Esther and the girls, bringing along with them whatever they had on hand to feed the searchers — pies, bread, roasts, hams, fruits and vegetables. It seemed to Esther that there were a hundred people in the house, with more coming in and stumping out all the time, but in reality the number was not even half that.

It had been agreed that positively no shots would be fired unless the boy was found. If he should be brought in, then a series of five shots each would be fired at intervals until all the searchers had come in. But throughout the stormy night the search continued and no shots were fired.

A massive breakfast was prepared at dawn and eaten by the drenched searchers as they showed up at the house to check in and then go out again. And with each new arrival there was always a bombardment of the same questions:

"Find him?"

"Did you get Ben?"

"Any *sign* of him at least?"

And always the answers were the same. No. Even George Burton, probably the most experienced tracker among them, was baffled.

"I reckon," he said on one of his stops at the house, not realizing how close to the truth he came, "I reckon the boy took out either straight up or straight down, 'cause sure t'God he ain't nowheres 'round on the ground here'bouts. An' they ain't no trace of him no-how, nowhere."

Esther, with Coral and Beth close beside her, was pale and drawn and mostly she sat quietly, waiting. Just waiting. And in the eyes of those who glanced her way and then quickly averted their gaze, she read their growing lack of hope, their sympathy. She refused to acknowledge either. Somewhere out there was her little Ben, still alive, perhaps crying for her, waiting for help. They had to find him. They *had* to.

They didn't.

The rigors of the search began to tell on them. Eyes became grainy and red from lack of sleep; unshaven men rubbed their stubbly chins and shook their heads sadly at one another. Yet, still they searched. Throughout the day and into the second night of heavy rains they continued to look, their lanterns bobbing with an eerie glow far out in the desolate prairies. Some came in about midnight of the second night and flopped in exhaustion on the floor in the house or out in the barn, but after an hour or so they would be up and out again. Two nights and two days they searched and it was not until near sunset of the second day, when the rain had eased off and the air had become still, that five shots in succession rang out from the MacDonalds' yard. Searchers far out on the prairie hills heard it and they sighed gratefully and turned their horses in that direction.

William MacDonald was one of the farthest away and one of the weariest, not having closed his eyes, eaten, or rested since the search began, but he kneed the equally weary Dover into a halfhearted gallop toward home when the sound of the shots reached him ever so faintly.

Practically everyone was clustered before the house on Hawk's Hill when he rode in. The murmur of conversation stilled and all eyes were directed his way. There were no smiles.

"He's been found?" MacDonald shouted, leaping from the horse and running toward them. "Is he all right? Where was he?"

Esther ran up to meet him and flung her arms around him, burying her face in his shirtfront and shaking her head. "They didn't find him, Will. They didn't find Ben."

MacDonald's face became suffused with anger and he glared across the faces. "Who fired?" he demanded. "Who fired that gun when Ben hadn't been found?"

Joe Billington stepped forward. In contrast to his rangy sons, he was a short, heavy, oaken-barrel sort of man.

" 'Twas my shots you heard, William MacDonald," he said. "I meant 'em to call you in. It's no use any more, man. The boy's gone."

"You're . . . quitting the search?" MacDonald seemed bewildered.

"Aye. There's no more use. We've talked it over among us. If there was any hint, any faint suggestion that still he lived, even if there was only a clue about which direction he went, we'd search on. But you have to face it, man, there's not been that first wee sign of your boy."

MacDonald started to speak but Billington stopped him with a gesture. He was grimly sorrowful. "I know how you're feeling, MacDonald. I'd feel the same were it one of mine. But look, man, you've thirty-two searchers here, counting yourself and John. And we've all been looking steadily for two nights and two days. And in all that time, all that ground covered, there hasn't been that first little sign of him. We figure there's only one thing that can mean: the river. He must've fallen in and been swept away without a trace left behind. MacDonald, no man of us'd think of leaving you if there was hope; but there is just no hope! I'm sorry."

Robert McKinzie, a tall, sturdy man with hair almost white, though he could not have been much over fifty, spoke up now. He had been MacDonald's neighbor for eighteen years and probably was closer to him than any of the others. But McKinzie, too, had no hope.

"Afraid he's right, William. Without any sign on the ground anywhere of Ben, the likeliest thing is that the boy went down by the Red and somehow tumbled in. If so, God only knows where he might be by now. The way the river's gone into low flood with this weather, he could've been washed clear down to the lake by this time." He paused, then added, "We're sorry, William, all of us. We've done our best but there's just no more use in hunting. One of us would've found sign of him somewhere if he'd been out there." He swept an arm out, indicating the prairies.

MacDonald had begun shaking his head as Joe Billington was talking and had continued to shake it at intervals until now. He knew he should be grateful for all the help they'd been, for the enormous effort they had expended in this search, but all he could think of now was that they were deserting him, leaving him without help and even trying to take away his hope. His and Esther's. He shook his head a final time and his voice was tight with bitterness.

"You're wrong," he said, "all of you. Esther and I, John and the girls, we thank you for your help, but we can't accept that he's gone. Go on home if you want. We'll keep on looking. Ben's somewhere and we'll find him."

There was nothing more to say. A few in the crowd were mildly irked that this Scotsman should be so ungrateful after all their efforts, but mostly they understood and sympathized with him and Esther. But the reality of the situation was clear: it was not their fault that Ben was lost and that he had not been found. They had searched long and hard and it was highly unfair to expect them to go on searching indefinitely. And yet, in the majority of them this justification still left a bitter taste and they carried with them a sense of embarrassment, even guilt, as they turned away and climbed into their buggies and wagons or straddled their horses and filed away down the rutted trail.

They stood and watched them go, William and Esther MacDonald, aware that John, Beth and Coral were watching them silently from the porch. William put his arm around her at last and gently turned her toward the house. He was dejected, but not beaten.

"Ben's not dead, Esther," he told her softly. "He had to go somewhere and somewhere there has to be a trace of where he went. Tomorrow's another day and we'll keep on looking. We'll find him. We won't quit until we do."

Chapter 10

By the time the rain began on the second evening, Ben was inside the roomy den chamber and asleep. He had shaken the dirt out of his makeshift trouser-bag and then put the pants back on for warmth. At the moment he lay curled on his side and even though he had thrown some of the grasses over himself in an effort to keep warm, still he shivered in his sleep and occasionally moaned or cried out unintelligibly.

Though the rain falling outside could not be heard, here and there droplets fell into the den area with monotonous persistence. Evening turned into night and about an hour after full darkness had fallen there was a wheezing in the main tunnel and the female badger came cautiously into view. Had Ben been awake he would have had difficulty seeing her in this darkness, but her own vision was such that she could see him reasonably well, and she stood quietly looking at his curled form for a considerable while. An almost inaudible whine came from her and she shook herself vigorously twice, then came forward and touched the boy's arm with her nose. He did not wake.

She whined faintly again and squeezed into the narrow gap between the boy and the den wall. Ben felt her and opened his eyes, momentarily startled at her presence there; but her nearness and warmth were strangely comforting and after a while he snuggled closer to her and put an arm over her. She tensed slightly, then relaxed and whined again, but there was no sound from Ben. He had already gone back to sleep.

Shortly before dawn the badger stirred and pulled out from under his arm. He did not awaken as she left the den and he was still asleep when she returned, though it had been daylight for more than an hour. She came close to him and made a guttural chattering sound, touched his cheek with her nose and then stepped back a little when his eyes fluttered and opened. It was much lighter in the den chamber now.

"I'm glad you came back, badger," he said. He sat up and yawned and then reached a hand out to pat her. This time she did not flinch at all and after a moment she dipped her head and opened her mouth. A buff-colored egg rolled out. A few brown spots near the smaller end of the shell were darkened by her saliva. It was a little smaller than a hen's egg.

For a moment Ben couldn't believe it. There was the weird conviction in his mind, during those first few seconds, that she had actually laid the egg from her mouth. Hunger overcame amazement and he picked up the egg greedily, recognizing it now as a prairie chicken egg. He wanted no drop of it to be wasted, so he picked up his rock chip from the den floor and

146

gently tapped the speckled end of the egg until it buckled. It was just as well that he could not make out details too clearly in the dimness of this chamber, for the egg was about halfway along in its development to a chick, with a soft but decidedly recognizable embryo.

He opened the shell enough so that the insides could come out and then held the opening to his mouth and tilted his head back. The contents slid into his mouth and almost before he realized it he had swallowed. He blinked and then grinned.

"Didn't even chew, badger," he said.

He stuck his tongue into the hole but the inside was empty and he tossed the eggshell to one side and then watched with interest as the badger came close to him and sat down. He stroked her fur and she moved even closer to him. She licked his cheek several times and then, even as he continued to pat her, she lay down and rolled over onto her side, exposing her milk-swollen nipples to him. At first he didn't understand but then it dawned on him that she wished to suckle him, as he had seen the ewes suckle their lambs. He wondered if he should, even thought for just an instant that he might try; but, hungry though he was, the idea of it was just too much for him and he shook his head. He patted her stomach, stroked the long fur some more and gently rubbed the rounded ears, but he remained sitting upright.

After a little while she rolled back over and sat up. She grunted and chattered, a sound he mimicked immediately, and she picked up the empty eggshell in her mouth and disappeared down the main burrow with it. He hesitated, then followed her, but by the time he reached the surface, she was gone.

The night's rain had cleansed and replenished the water supply in the depression of the rock. He drank deeply and then he crawled over to the rock pile, moved around it halfway and prepared to move his bowels. While perched on his heels, he gazed around and was alarmed to see not just one but three horsemen in different directions, though none of them very near to him. He quickly finished, cleansed himself with a handful of grass and rehitched his pants. In seconds he was back within the hole and only his head and shoulders still remained sticking out as he continued to observe.

His alarm this time was not for himself — not with this haven of the den right beneath him — but instead for the badger should she be seen by one of these men. Visions of the dead animal Burton had brought to Hawk's Hill filled his mind and he relived again the awful feel of the squashiness of the dead badger's skull under his touch, from the crushing blow Burton had struck it with his club. He was sick with the fear that the same would happen to his notch-eared companion.

He needn't have worried. The female badger was no bumbling youngster. She was highly skilled in the ability to travel the prairie unseen if need be. The very squatness of her body kept her low to the ground, below the level of the grasses if she so chose. Nevertheless, Ben was frightened. And when one of the riders turned in his direction, even though the better part of a mile away, he swiftly ducked back down the hole and returned to the den chamber where he sat and trembled.

About twenty minutes later the female badger returned, bearing another prairie chicken egg. He took it off the den floor where she had placed it and ate it just as he had eaten the first. His enjoyment of it was no less. She left him again and half an hour later was back with a third egg. By midday she had brought a total of eight eggs to him and he had eaten them all in turn. Knowing that the prairie chicken normally had twelve to fourteen eggs, he assumed that she had eaten some herself at the nest and he wondered if it was the nest of the bird that he had eaten.

The next time the badger returned to the den she carried in her mouth not an egg but a large prairie garter snake. This offering, too, she put on the den floor before him, but he would not take it and when she realized this, she settled down and devoured it herself.

Ben lay on his side watching her as she ate, but he had fallen asleep again before she was finished. She curled beside him as she had on the previous night and almost automatically his arm came up to lie across her and keep her snugly against him.

A pattern was being established between them and both fell into it with remarkable ease. In the days which followed she did most of her hunting by night and when, in the morning, he would awaken, always there would be a new morsel on the floor for him. Once it was a chipmunk and another time it was a molting adult gadwall duck. Twice in a row she brought prairie chickens and, as he had done with the duck, he cut and chopped them apart with his sharp rock chip, giving her the head, intestines and internal organs, wings and feet, and himself eating the meat of breast and legs. Several times she returned with mice and had his hunger not been intense the first time, after a fast of fifteen hours, he would have rejected the offering. But he put distaste aside and ripped away the skin, giving it and the head, feet, tail and entrails back to her, then ate the meat himself. He found to his surprise and delight that it was not unpleasant at all and so when she brought others back to the den, he cleaned and ate them without further hesitation. Twice she brought back large dripping chunks of honeycomb in her mouth and once even a fair-sized hunk of bread that someone had evidently dropped on the trail.

Though the relationship between boy and badger had begun simply as one of food and shelter, it did not remain that way. A deep affection was developing between them and a spirit of play as well. During the first week Ben stayed underground almost all the time, coming to the surface only rarely to drink or relieve himself. The availability of drinking water for Ben always seemed to be a looming hazard, for the level in the rock depression lowered with each drink he took.

Twice he had licked it dry, only to fortuitously have it refilled both times by another rainstorm.

After the first week, Ben began to venture outside with her more often, always copying her movements, mimicking her grunts and wheezes, imitating her hissings and chatterings and snorts, even able to emulate with remarkable accuracy her waddling, flowing gait. Rarely did he stand erect and then only to briefly look about himself for possible danger before dropping back to all fours.

Frequently they played a sort of tag. She would run from him and he would scramble after her through the tall grasses, panting and giggling at one point, wheezing and chattering at another. And when at last he would catch her — or she would *let* him catch her — he would tackle her around the middle and they would roll over and over together, their snarlings and growlings of mock battle intermingling. Suddenly it would be his turn and he would dash away with her closing in behind him and she would pounce upon him in much the same manner and once again they would wrestle amidst giggles and chatterings.

It had been at the end of this third day with her that Ben noticed she seemed to be favoring her injured foot even more than previously. As she stretched out on the den floor he sat beside her and gently raised her foot. She whined at first and made a slight effort to pull away, but he maintained a gentle grip and looked at the injury closely. The pad of the foot was very badly swollen and hot to the touch. A serous fluid was barely oozing from two small openings in the scabrous material covering the wound.

He left her and went to the puddle, soaked one of his socks in it and came back down to her. She had not moved and except for a slightly heavy breathing, made no sound when he took her paw and daubed it at length with the wet cloth. He was able to clean away the grit and dirt, but the crusty scabrous material was stubborn. Abruptly he leaned over and spat on the wound, let the warm sputum stay there for a minute or two and then daubed it with the cloth. A little bit of the scabbing came off and he tried it again. Once more a small particle broke free, but the process was too slow for him.

Just as she had frequently licked his face and hands, so now he leaned over and began licking her paw. Gradually the crusty surface softened and flaked off or melted away and before long only the tender wound edge remained. Now he put her paw between the heels of his thumbs and applied a gentle but increasing pressure. She whined a bit and he could feel her body trembling beside him, but she made no effort to pull away. And then, from first one and then the other of the two spots which had been oozing, there was a sudden little burst of dark reddish fluid interspersed with little strands and gobs of pus. He wiped it away thoroughly with the damp sock and squeezed again, repeating the process three or four times until nothing more came from the cavity but a minute amount of clear fluid.

There was no way whatever for him to bandage it, nor would she have been likely to leave a bandage in place had he been able to fashion one. Nevertheless, the wound improved. For five days running he repeated the process of cleansing, licking and squeezing and at the end of that time a good healthy skin was forming. And to Ben's delight, he soon had good evidence that she was regaining the use of this foot in her hunting. The first evidence was on the morning of the sixth day, when she returned to the den with another chipmunk and with the hairs between her toes of both front feet clotted with mud from her digging. The second and more conclusive evidence came on the twelfth night when she returned with a fine large Franklin's ground squirrel which she had quite evidently dug up from deep in its burrow.

By the beginning of his third week with her, Ben was astonishingly badger-like in all he did. He could keep up with her reasonably well and he grunted and wheezed as he waddled along, just as she did. He was no longer so particular about what he would eat and devoured with equal alacrity any prey she brought to him, including frogs and lemmings and once even a small red-bellied snake.

Nor was he content any more to remain in the den while she went off on her nightly hunting. He began following her, watching from the deep grasses as she sometimes caught prey on the surface, or coming close to her as she dug swiftly downward — though no longer as swiftly as she once could — after chipmunks and spermophiles and other ground squirrels. His night vision was becoming extremely good and he almost seemed to prefer it to daylight. His mental clock became turned around and, like the female badger, he slept most of the day and was alert most of the night.

Now and then, especially in the solitude of the den when she was not with him, thoughts of his home and family would flood him and he would break out in sobs, but such occasions became ever fewer as time progressed.

There was no doubt that the big female badger had adopted him in place of her pups which had died while she was trapped. It was evident that she was bringing food to him and attempting to train him in hunting just as she would have done her own young. It was considerably more difficult, however, to understand the change in the boy. Except in his habits of defecation and urination, Ben MacDonald had virtually ceased being a human being and was adapting incredibly well to this life of a badger.

Water for Ben's consumption was no longer a real problem. Three-fourths of a mile from their burrow was a small pothole with far more water than he could use and they began going there regularly. Here also, sliding easily through the reedy shallows, he delighted in catching frogs — the one prey he had no difficulty with — and sharing them with her. But on their fifth journey together to the pothole, they encountered more than merely frogs.

They left the den an hour after nightfall, but the grass tops were silvered by the glow of a full moon and Ben could see well for a considerable distance. It was a pleasant, balmy night and Ben was in a playful mood. He tugged several times at the badger's tail as she waddled along ahead of him toward the distant pothole. This was usually the way their romping and tussling began. But on this night she seemed preoccupied and ignored his little teasings, and Ben realized she sensed something that was bothering her.

The panting wheeze that often accompanied her walking was absent, though occasionally she issued the faintest of grunts and growls, so softly voiced that Ben himself could barely hear them. From the way she was acting, Ben surmised that she herself did not know precisely what was wrong, for she paused frequently to raise her muzzle and sniff. Not until they were nearly to the pothole did her low growl rise in timbre and her teeth gleam whitely in the moonlight as her lip curled in a full snarl. At this time they had been just about to leave the area of deep grass to cross an encircling area of low-green marshy ground around the pothole. Suddenly, emulating the female, Ben crouched and froze, still hidden in the final fringe of these deeper grasses. She was more exposed and though he could not see what had alarmed her, he could sense her trembling ahead of him and he followed the direction of her gaze.

Only when an echoing, deep-throated growl came from the reed fringe did he see the peril. There, crouching low and facing them, camouflaged by the pattern of shadows from the moonlit reeds falling over his back, was the big yellow-gray mongrel, Lobo. He had obviously seen the badger, but apparently not the boy behind her. His fangs, much larger than the badger's, were exposed in a terrible snarl and Ben felt a shudder ripple through him. He waited tensely, shivering, expecting Lobo to charge the badger. Instead, it was the badger who suddenly split the air with a hair-raising snarling growl that was almost a shriek and hurled herself headlong at this foe.

Lobo held his ground and then at the last moment he met her charge with his own chilling variety of viciousness. They clinched, standing on their hind feet, grasping each other with forelegs and teeth, but it was the much greater weight of the dog which prevailed. His near ninety pounds of muscle thrust her over onto her back and she went down shrieking and clawing and biting. For a while the struggle was so intense, so fast-moving, so shifting, that Ben could make no judgment about who was winning. There was a macabre, prehistoric unreality to the scene which stirred him to his deepest fiber and caused the hair on his own nape to tighten and tingle.

Abruptly the badger broke free and spun around, raising her short tail as she did so and secreting a strong musk in the direction of the dog. It was not as powerful a musk as that which the badger's weasel relative, the skunk, could eject, nor could she shoot it as accurately or as far as the skunk, but it was nonetheless a vile-smelling oily liquid and a terrible irritant to the eyes. Had it gotten into Lobo's eyes, it would have temporarily blinded him and he would have been more vulnerable to her next attack. But none of the musk struck the dog and now it was he who charged her. He came at her in an arcing thrust, trying to catch her exposed flank. Driving in low, he missed her side but somehow managed to get his snout beneath her and flip her.

Until that moment everywhere his teeth had closed on her the grizzled fur was so dense and her skin so loose that she was able to pull away from him before he could cause any serious damage. But in being flipped this way, her throat was momentarily exposed. In that fragment of time, he had her. She gave a hideously strangled cry as the fangs locked on her and, as he bore her to the ground on her back, the fearsome claws of both her front and hind feet tore frenziedly at his underside in an effort to disembowel. Long dark stains began streaking the big dog's belly and flanks and his continuing growl had become as much from pain as from fury. But through it all he maintained his grip and exerted more and more pressure to drive his great canine teeth deeper into her.

Suddenly there was another chattering growl as Ben streaked forward on all fours from his hiding place and threw himself on Lobo's rear. With one hand he gripped the dog's tail and with the other a hind leg. It may have been accidental or it may have been the result of a primitive instinct from deep in some remote, primeval corner of his brain directing it, but

whichever was the case he drove his open, snarling mouth down onto the Achilles tendon of the leg he was holding, feeling the toughness of that thick sinew between his teeth and exerting every ounce of pressure his jaws could muster in the bite.

The surprise, the agonizing pain and the hazard of this rear attack caused Lobo to relinquish his hold on the badger and wheel to face his new adversary. But the dog was badly off balance now and the ravaging teeth which snapped together at the boy missed his flesh and caught only the shoulder of his sleeve and ripped it down its length. Ben did not relinquish his hold and in Lobo's new concentration on him, the dog forgot for a fatal instant the big female badger.

She had regained her feet and now she catapulted into him and this time it was her teeth which found the mark. They closed low on Lobo's throat and instantly she braced all four feet against him and tore wrenchingly, the thrust of her feet adding even greater tearing strength to her jaws.

The growling from Lobo changed abruptly to a terrified shriek and his legs scrabbled as he tried desperately to wrest himself away. It was too late. The incredible strength of the badger, the fierceness with which she bit and pushed simultaneously was too much. The skin of Lobo's throat tore and the great jugular held for just an instant longer and then it too tore open. Immediately all three combatants were bathed in a gush of blood and the grass and ground became slippery with it.

Lobo's strength rapidly dwindled but not until the dog lay limp in her teeth did the badger release her grip on his throat. Ben had already let go and was half-sprawled on the spongy ground, stunned by all that had happened and trembling violently. The badger whined softly and came to him, nuzzling him and licking his face. He put his arms around her and leaned his head against hers and suddenly he was crying.

When she pulled out of his grasp and went back to the dead dog, again growling ominously, he followed her and growled as she did. But when she made as if to leave, he hesitated. If the dog should be found here, George Burton was sure to come with traps or guns to destroy whatever killed Lobo. And so, despite the badger's insistent chattering at him, he gripped the dog by the hind legs and, on his knees, backed into the densest portion of the cattail reeds, pulling Lobo after him. He was in water to his waist when he finally let go of the dead animal. Its head and hindquarters were under water but its left side, buoyed with the air locked in its body, was still afloat.

Twice Ben thumped the exposed side of the carcass with his small fist and a small amount of air was forced out. While the remains no longer floated so high, still they floated. He didn't know what else to do so he merely bent a number of the surrounding reeds over until they draped across the dog's body and fairly well masked it. Then he backed out onto the marshy ground again, pushing upright the reeds he had disturbed, and when he was finished it would have been difficult to detect that anyone had gone in there.

They went back to the burrow then, the badger and the boy. In its shelter, as another thunderstorm boomed outside, the boy found the several places where Lobo's teeth had punctured her skin and he licked them clean for her. Ben himself had suffered no injury.

They had nothing to eat that night or the next day, but on the following evening they were out hunting together again and by morning they had shared in eating four jumping mice, a lemming, a leopard frog and a fledgling pintail duck.

As the days and nights continued, however, a subtle but fundamental change was taking place in Ben. Though the female badger seemed to thrive on their relationship, Ben's physical condition had begun deteriorating. He had come to the burrow during the last week of June; by the middle of July he had become well ensconced in his new wild existence, and as the August moon waxed and then began to wane, his metamorphosis was almost complete. But as mid-August passed and the days of that month dwindled, he became increasingly lethargic. Only infrequently would he play and wrestle with the big female badger and he no longer cared to travel long distances with her to hunt. When, after hunting alone one night, she returned to the den before dawn with a large fat prairie dog — her first such prey since before her tragedy — he was content to remain in the den until it was all gone, alternately feeding on it and sleeping and going no farther from the den than the pothole in order to drink when the supply in the basin-shaped rock became depleted.

Thin and slight he might have been before, but now he was becoming practically skeletal. His eyes had acquired an unhealthy brightness and often he moaned in his sleep. It was clear that he was becoming quite unwell. Unless something occurred to change matters — and very soon at that — Benjamin MacDonald was apt to become just as dead as the majority of people in this area of the Manitoba prairie country thought him to be.

Chapter 11

Even though the MacDonald family had reluctantly attended the memorial services held for Ben in North Corners ten days after the boy's disappearance, neither Esther nor William truly believed their youngest son to be dead. Now, two months after he had vanished, they still refused to accept this conclusion.

Esther had become pale, gaunt, tight-lipped from the emotional strain of these days and weeks during which she had eaten little and slept restlessly at best. William MacDonald, if anything, looked even worse than she. For the first week after Benjamin's disappearance he had been in the saddle upwards of twenty hours a day. For three days and nights he was gone from home entirely as he followed the Red River slowly down the west bank all the way to its outlet in Lake Winnipeg, swam his horse across there and came back up the other side. He found no trace of Ben.

John looked bad, too, but unlike his parents he had come to the conclusion that his little brother was dead, a conclusion that he had thus far kept to himself. Though he continued to search as diligently as his father, what John looked for was not a living little brother but rather some sort of specific evidence that Ben was dead. He shuddered as he thought of his parents going through the rest of their lives with the forlorn hope deep within them that somewhere, somehow, Ben still lived.

Until the disappearance, John MacDonald had been just a normal boy of sixteen, but these past two months had wrought changes for him also, helping to instill in him a maturity far beyond his years. He had become a serious young man instead of merely a carefree boy. Without complaint he had shouldered much more than his share of work around the farm. When his chores were finished each day, he grimly saddled his mare, Dilly, and rode long hours, searching. These days when he searched he rarely looked far ahead since he no longer harbored the hope of seeing his little brother at a distance. Instead, he scanned the ground closely, watching for anything at all that might indicate Ben had been here; hopeful for a glimpse of a bit of cloth from his clothing and constantly depressed by his vision of inevitably finding Ben's bones.

Even his mother and the girls continued to search, especially relatively close to the house. Knowing only too well the frailty and timidity of her last-born, Esther had convinced herself that Ben would be found within half a mile of the house and her searching in this area — aided by Coral and Beth — was perhaps the most intensive of all.

To keep from going over the same ground twice,

once all of the buildings had been checked beyond any possibility of Ben being in them, she carried a sack of flour with her and every thirty feet or so she would strew a handful of it across the tops of the grasses to mark where the search had been and where next it needed to go. With Coral just over an arm's length to her left and Beth the same distance to the left of Coral, they walked in a counterclockwise spiral around the farm, gradually expanding the ring of their passage on the slopes of Hawk's Hill and remaining outside the flour trail Esther was leaving. When Coral would grow too weary to search more, Esther would send her and Beth back to the house to rest and she would continue the circling search herself. But the results were always the same: nothing. It was as if what George Burton had said was true, that Ben must have gone either straight up or straight down, because there was no evidence of him on ground level. At least that was how it seemed at this beginning of the last week in August.

The greatest single difficulty everyone experienced in the search was the inability to judge with any real degree of certainty the direction Ben had taken when he left. Had that one fact been ascertained, heavy efforts could have been concentrated in that direction. But with no clue whatever in that respect, they could only try to guess which direction the boy had taken and the immensity of the area this might include was appalling. Unfortunately, their best reckonings thus far in this respect had been in error. First choice of everyone was toward the river, and even though the area between house and river — as well as the river-banks themselves — had been assiduously scoured without success, this direction still ranked high in all their minds as the probable one Ben had taken. Second in likelihood, to their way of thinking, was toward the meandering little stream known as Wolf Creek, which left the forest lands ten miles to the north and wove its way southeastward through the prairied hill country and passed two miles to the north of Hawk's Hill before emptying into the Red River.

The area most heavily dotted with potholes was to the northwest of the farm. This was their third choice. For more than a week both William and John had come home each evening utterly exhausted, their skin wrinkled and their clothing wet and muddy from one after another plunging through the reed-cloaked pot-holes to search each one thoroughly.

Now, in this eighth week of search, John had moved off to the southwest of the farm. His eyes burned from staring at the ground and at the grasses swishing by beneath his mare. After a while it all grew to look the same, as if he were riding in an endless circle and seeing the same ground over and over; buffalo grass mostly, a patch of lower grass here and there, a scattered rock or two pushed above the ground surface by last winter's freezes, now and then a stretch of relatively barren ground.

When it happened, he very nearly didn't see it. To his weary eyes the lump in the grasses registered as just another small rock pushing upward. In fact, he had gone a dozen feet or more past it when he suddenly frowned and reined his horse in. He dismounted, giving Dilly a chance to rest and graze a bit as he walked stiffly back to stand over it. With his eyes nearer to it now and with his attention specifically centered on it, he stared unbelievingly at the object and wondered for an instant how he could have nearly mistaken it for a rock. With a little cry he fell to his knees and picked it up.

Mold-covered from resting for so long beneath the damp grasses, it was nevertheless unmistakably Ben MacDonald's right shoe. Almost reverently John hugged it to him and then held it out again to stare at it wonderingly. After all this time, after all these endless, unrewarded hours and days and weeks of searching, a clue at last!

His first thought was to mark the place and he peered around anxiously for anything that might be used. There was nothing but grass and rolling hills. He shucked off his light jacket and dropped it in a pile on the precise spot where the shoe had been. Then he went back to Dilly and from the saddle scabbard he withdrew the rifle of which he was so proud — a .22 caliber Wesson breechloader made by the Folsom Company of Chicago — which had been given to him as a birthday present last March.

He went back to his jacket with the firearm and without a second thought he rammed the barrel deep into the ground so that the stock was sticking into the air well above the grasses. Over this he hung his jacket, tying the sleeves together so it would not blow off. This marker, he knew, could be seen from a considerable distance. Then he began circling the spot on foot, searching intently. Within twenty minutes he found the left shoe, more hidden than the first had been and about forty or fifty feet to the west of where the coat-draped rifle was sticking up. A low bush was growing here and John tied his big handkerchief to one of the uppermost branches.

The youth glanced up at the cloudless sky. It was still about an hour before noon. He wished now that he had fired the gun before ramming it into the ground. Both father and he had agreed to shoot three times if anything was found indicating Ben might have been in the area. He shrugged, guessing it really didn't matter that much, considering their plan this morning: father had headed straight west from the house after breakfast to search in that direction, while John had angled southwest, and they planned to head toward one another beginning about noon. Though as yet John could not see the elder MacDonald, he was sure his father would probably show up within the next couple of hours. In the meanwhile, John determined to keep searching.

He returned to the mare and mounted, then sat there for a moment planning his moves. The rifle marker and handkerchief tied to the bush were in a straight east-west line from one another, giving reasonable indication that Ben had been moving in that line. The problem was, in which direction? There was no way of telling. The slope of the ground here was a gentle rise to the east and John found it easier to surmise that Ben had been going downhill, and so he turned his horse to the west.

He held Dilly to a slow walk, angling back and forth over the supposed line of Ben's path. Occasionally he raised his eyes to look ahead, but the only break nearby in the rippling blanket of buffalo grass was a low outcropping of rocks still about a hundred yards ahead. He considered it. That might be just the sort of thing which would have attracted Ben and so John continued his zigzagging course in that direction.

Abruptly a wildly clucking sharp-tailed grouse burst from the grasses just in front of the horse and rocketed away. Dilly reared and whinnied in sudden fright but John kept the saddle and managed to get her under control. The sudden noise made by both bird and horse, however, had evidently frightened something else. Even as he fought to maintain his seat and regain control of the mare, John peripherally saw movement far ahead and turned his gaze to glimpse a low dark shape speeding through the grasses. The mare turned a complete circle and by the time he could see well again in that direction, John just barely spotted the shape disappearing near the rock pile.

He shook his head, puzzled. His first thought was that it had been a badger or wolverine, but on further consideration he rejected both ideas, though he wasn't sure in his own mind why except that somehow the impression just seemed wrong. He similarly rejected the possibility of black bear, wolf or coyote; all three of which would almost certainly have kept going. Frowning, he kneed the mare forward, dismounted some fifty feet from the rocks, and let Dilly's reins trail. He suddenly found himself wishing he had his rifle, and his hand went automatically to his right hip. He was somewhat comforted by the feel of the heavy-bladed sheath knife there, but still he wished he had the gun. A nine-foot braided rawhide whip was coiled and tied on the outside of the rifle scabbard and he debated taking it along but then moved off without it.

He stepped along quietly, watching the ground ahead of him carefully, but even then he was almost upon the big hole before he saw it. There was no sign of life around it but he was convinced that whatever the thing had been, it was in that burrow. The hole angled inward beside a flat rock with a little bit of rainwater residue still in a small natural basin on top.

Noting the direction in which the hole was angling, John carefully moved around until he was about twenty feet behind it. There he crouched in the grasses and waited quietly. He tried to reason out what the thing he glimpsed could have been and why, regardless of what it was, he was taking the time to sit here waiting it out when he should be searching for further sign of Ben. He didn't *know* why, but somehow he just couldn't make himself get up and leave.

Half an hour passed and John's patience was running thin. Had he been wrong about whatever it was having gone into this hole? Mightn't it have kept going and run off unseen, keeping the rock pile between itself and John? His doubts increased and he was on the point of getting on with his search when there was the faintest suggestion of movement at the hole and he stiffened.

Little by little something was emerging and suddenly John's eyes widened and his mouth gaped in astonishment. It was human! The head became exposed even more, facing in the opposite direction, and then the arms came out and raised the form higher in order to see over the grass. The head turned slowly and provided John with a profile view and the youth blinked with total amazement.

It was Ben!

Though the boy's hair was wildly unkempt and matted with dirt, his face muddy and his lips cracked, there could be no doubt that it was Ben. The boy, now exposed to the waist, had just seen the horse and seemed on the verge of ducking back into the hole. Still overwhelmed, John leaped up and rushed toward him.

"Ben! Ben! It's me, John."

There was a momentary shocked glance from the boy and then he was gone. An instant later John was kneeling over the hole, his head in the opening, and he was calling to his little brother.

"Ben, don't you know me? It's John, Ben. Your brother. Come on out, you're safe now. I won't hurt you, Ben. Don't be afraid."

From within the depths of the burrow came a series of spine-chilling snarls and growls and hissings. John grimaced and jerked his knife from the sheath and began enlarging the hole, scooping out the loosened earth with his free hand. He had gotten no more than his shoulders into the hole when suddenly Ben came charging up the passage, spitting and snarling viciously and intent upon clawing the intruder's face.

The youth snatched and caught one of the thin wrists and jerked backward, pulling the boy up after him. And now, fully exposed, Ben attacked him in earnest, grappling with him, ripping at him with his long toenails and clawing at his face with his fingernails. His teeth sank deeply into the back of the hand gripping his wrist, but John did not let go.

"Ben!" he shouted. "For God's sake, Ben, stop it. I'm John. *Stop it!*"

The words had no effect and the boy continued struggling wildly. John managed to pin both arms firmly with one of his and hug Ben's back firmly to his own chest and in this way he picked the little boy up and headed for the mare who was staring nervously at them. But John was only thirty feet away from the hole when a new snarling made him spin around and he blanched. An enormous badger had erupted from the hole and was charging at him with unmistakably murderous ferocity.

He turned and ran with his struggling burden and murmured a silent thanks for the steadfastness of Dilly,

172

who, while decidedly frightened, held her ground at his approach with the fiercely fighting child in his arms and the even more fiercely snarling badger not far behind him. John reached the horse only a dozen feet ahead of the female badger and he snatched the whip from the saddle and lashed out at her. It was swung more than cracked and it was definitely not a damaging blow, but his hasty aim had been good and it thumped painfully across her muzzle, momentarily tangled her front feet, and partially tumbled her.

By the time she had regained her equilibrium and charged anew, John had vaulted into the saddle with Ben. With the trailing whip in the same hand that was gripping the reins and the other arm firmly pinning Ben to his own chest, John jerked the mare into a gallop. Still growling and furiously shrieking, the badger followed but she was quickly outdistanced.

In addition to the bite on his hand, John's shirt sleeve was torn and his upper arm was bleeding where the boy's teeth had managed momentarily to grip him as he was mounting the horse, but now all the fire seemed to have gone out of the child and he slumped in John's grasp, almost a deadweight. With the mare still running flat out, John caught sight of a horseman far in the distance to the northwest coming toward him and he angled his own steed in that direction.

It was William MacDonald, and though from such a distance he could not make out detail, he knew it had to be John and the fact that the approaching horse was in a full gallop could only mean something important had happened. He urged his own mount into a hard run.

In his great excitement, John began shouting when they were still three hundred yards apart and he didn't stop until they reined in their horses.

"Dad!" he cried. "Dad, it's Ben. I found Ben! I've got him, Dad, and he's all right. *Ben's all right!*"

The elder MacDonald was practically overcome. Tears flowed unashamedly down his cheeks and at first all he could say was, "Oh, thank God, thank God, thank God . . ."

He drew Dover up beside John's mare and tried to take the boy from his older son, but now Ben did a turnabout and snarled viciously at his father, then twisted around so his face was buried in John's shirt and his little arms gripped his brother around the waist with surprising strength and determination. Muffled growls still came from him and John looked helplessly at his father.

Even greater reaction was hitting the older man. He bent his head and his shoulders heaved with the depth of his weeping. John had never seen his father cry — not even at Ben's disappearance or later on at the memorial service — and the sight of it, even more than the joy in finding Ben, choked him up as well and the tears coursed freely down his cheeks.

After a moment, his head still bowed, William MacDonald put his hands together and his words, when he spoke, were erratic and muffled, broken with emotion:

"Dear Lord . . . thank you for . . . preserving Ben and . . . thank you for delivering him to us."

His head remained down for a while longer and then he wiped his nose on the back of his hand and looked up. His smile almost made the older son break down again. He put his hand to John's shoulder and squeezed and the grip said more than any words could have.

"Come on, son," he said, "let's take Ben home to his mother."

Chapter 12

The reaction when the three MacDonalds reached the Hawk's Hill farm was no less emotional. Coral was first to see them coming and she stood before the house paralyzed with astonishment for a moment. Then the spell broke and she screamed piercingly.

"Mama! *Mama!*" She ran into the house still screaming. "It's Ben, mama, they found him! It's Ben, *and he's alive!*"

Coral raced back outside with Esther on her heels and Beth close behind them. They stopped in the middle of the yard, all three of them crying, and waited as the sweat-soaked horses plodded up and came to a stop. Esther, murmuring her youngest's name, reached up to take him from John. The little boy only clung tighter.

"Easy, Esther," William said gently. "He's all right. Let John get down with him. He's . . . scared."

She put a hand to her mouth and stepped back, suddenly alarmed without really knowing why. The whip was still trailing from John's grip and, realizing it, the older youth let it drop to the ground. MacDonald dismounted and took the reins from John, then reached up with one hand and helped him dismount with Ben. The elder MacDonald led the horses over to the nearby fence and looped the reins around the top rail. By the time he turned back, John had managed to get Ben's feet on the ground and disengage his grip. Ben crouched and backed away a little, like a wild animal at bay and snarling faintly.

Both Coral and Beth gasped and Esther moaned as if in pain. The child was in unspeakable condition. The wildness of his hair, now grown long and filthy, accentuated the furtive wildness in his eyes. His shirt was little more than rags and his trousers were even worse, with one leg ripped away at the knee and the other in tatters. He was barefooted and wherever his skin showed — face, neck, body, arms, legs and feet — he was grimy with dirt. His legs and arms were crisscrossed with scratches, some new, others in various stages of healing, and his lips were severely cracked. He was terribly thin, even more so than before, and he didn't look at all well. His eyes darted back and forth as if seeking some way to escape.

"Oh, Ben, Ben." Esther came forward to take him but he lurched back from her and startled her with a savage hissing growl and bared his teeth in a snarl. She looked at William helplessly.

"Let me, Mama." John stepped forward and stooped and held his arms out to Ben. A snarl met him but he came closer, still holding out his hands. Ben looked at the hands and then, for the first time, directly at John's face. The snarling stopped and he moved toward the older boy. Very carefully John touched Ben's arm and then slipped his own arm around the little boy's waist.

"Come on, Ben," he said softly, "you're home now. Let me take you inside."

He gathered his little brother into his arms and Ben clung tightly to him, once again hiding his face in John's shirtfront.

"I . . . don't understand," Esther murmured as she and William and the girls followed behind John into the house. "I . . . how . . . how could he stay alive so long by himself out there?"

MacDonald only shrugged. He had been pondering the same question and it just didn't seem possible.

John carried his brother into the parlor and put him down in the middle of the floor. When he disengaged Ben's grip and stepped back, again there was that momentary wild look in Ben's eyes. The boy darted glances at the tables and chairs, at the fireplace with the rifle and crossed swords hung over the mantel. He stared at the lamps and pictures and furnishings and then one by one at the people in the room. His nostrils dilated as he sniffed the smells once so familiar — spices and fresh bread, meat cooking and warm milk.

The wild look faded and he frowned. His mouth opened and shut and then opened again. For a short while longer he stood there and then, as if a switch had suddenly been thrown, everything seemed to register at once. His face screwed up and he wailed and

then stumbled toward Esther crying "Mama . . . Mama . . . Mama . . ."

She hugged him to her, lifting him up and rocking back and forth with him, murmuring to him and kissing him, the tears she shed falling on him and streaking his dirty skin. He clung to her with a sort of desperation, his own tears mingling with hers, and he made no effort now to shrink from the touches of the other members of the family as they crowded around and patted him and smiled . . . and wept.

It was MacDonald who expressed what all of them felt when he put his fingers under Ben's chin and tilted the boy's head to kiss the smudged cheek.

"Welcome home, Ben," he said. "Welcome home, son."

The day's excitement was far from over. Hardly had the family begun to regain its composure — as John was just telling them how he had fought off the badger by the hole — when from the doorway there came a new hissing and snarling. Wheezing and panting from her long run, her hackles standing upright as she glared and growled at them and curled her lips back from powerful teeth, the female badger crouched on the doorsill.

Both John and his father shouted warnings simultaneously. The girls screamed and drew back fearfully. In three steps MacDonald was at the fireplace and had snatched the heavy Henry repeating rifle from its pegs. Now it was Ben who screamed and even as his father raised the gun he jerked free from Esther's grasp and uttered a strange chattering sound as he ran to the badger and flung his arms around her neck, shielding her body with his own. The big animal licked his cheek briefly but continued the threatening growls directed at the family. MacDonald still held the gun poised to fire as soon as Ben should get out of the way, but now Esther moved to him and gently pushed the muzzle upward and shook her head.

"No, Will," she said. "I don't understand it, but she's Ben's. Or he's hers. Whichever, she's just trying to protect him. Look at them."

Ben, uttering a low, continuing chatter, was still hugging her around the neck with one arm, stroking her with his other hand, and had now leaned his head against hers. While still wheezing and grunting somewhat, the badger had settled down considerably, though it was still evident that she was extremely nervous being so near to these humans.

MacDonald nodded wonderingly and John muttered more to himself than to anyone else, "Who would have believed it?"

It was the beginning of an unusually difficult time of another sort, but little by little the female badger became a member of the MacDonald family. She would permit no other person than Ben to touch her, but with him she could not have been more gentle. The two were together constantly and Ben even refused to sleep in his bed, choosing instead to curl up with her on the floor in his bedroom and sleep with his arm protectively over her on the matting that had been provided for her.

Now it was Ben — cleaned and doctored and recuperating well under Esther's care — who cared for the badger, feeding her and protecting her as she had done for him at the den. She adapted remarkably well to his way of life. The door was always left open so that she could come and go as she pleased, but she always stayed near Ben and ate only what he gave her. At first she snarled frighteningly whenever anyone came near the boy, but Ben would chatter at her in a scolding manner and by the third day she seemed to have come to an acceptance of the fact that they meant no harm to him and she no longer bridled at their approach to him.

An understanding had quickly been reached in the family that they would let this matter run its course, whatever it might be. Esther was obsessed with the belief that if anything happened to the badger it would be Ben who suffered. As she told William late one night after the rest were asleep:

"I don't know *how* it'll end, Will. I don't have any idea. All I know is that we have Ben back now, and that's worth anything. If he wants to keep her as a pet until she falls dead with old age, then we'll let him. Oh, William, he's all tied up with her some way and we've got to try to understand, and even if we don't understand, we've got to try to help."

For a week Ben alternated between two lives, sometimes running around on all fours, growling, hissing, chattering and tussling with the badger as they played a sort of King-of-the-Hill game on the earth pile near the house where the well was being dug, and at other times talking with his family and acting like any other little boy his age. This was the thing most surprising to them, for Ben was now talking to them — all of them — as he never had before and it was obvious that he was enjoying the way they listened to him. For the first time in his life Ben had important things to say, things people were eager to hear. And what they wanted to know most, of course, were the details of what had happened during his absence.

He told them; not exactly chronologically perhaps, because it was all sort of muddled together to him, but he related incident after incident of his getting lost, of taking refuge from the storm in the badger hole, of his meeting with the animal — for the first time they learned how he had touched her initially in the prairie some time before his disappearance — and of her adoption of him.

He was pleased at their amazement when he told of cleansing her wounded paw by licking it and with their evident awe when he told how she had offered her milk to him and then, when he refused it, had brought him prairie chicken eggs and creatures she had caught. They managed not to appear too shocked when he told them of what he had eaten. And when he related how he had hidden from George Burton that first morning after the night's storm, not realizing that Burton was one member of the search party seeking him, they were better able to understand why no one had seen any sign of him after that, even though he had seen a number of horsemen. And it was much easier to understand, too, why he had fled at John's approach and even fought him when he was discovered.

What perhaps astounded them most was his story about the death of Lobo and, for the first time, they began to believe he was fabricating much of what he was telling them. How could their shy, extremely timid little son attack and bite a fearsome animal like that big yellow-gray dog; and that he and the badger together could have killed it was wholly beyond belief. But when John rode out to get his rifle where it was still stuck in the ground, he was gone a long time and he was wet when he returned. He took his parents aside and in an awed whisper told them he had gone to the pothole where Ben had said the fight took place. He had searched and finally found the decomposing body of the dog just where Ben had said it would be.

"I looked it over pretty well," John concluded, lowering his voice even more. "Mama, Dad . . . you wouldn't have believed it. The dog's throat was just ripped to shreds. And I looked at his hind leg, too, and it was bitten badly."

It was the last time they doubted what Ben told them.

As his accounts continued and expanded, the degree of vocabulary Ben possessed impressed and astounded them, especially in view of the fact that he had always been so monosyllabic in his speech before. It was evident now that while he had previously not spoken much he had listened much better than anyone thought and had learned from the family's conversation around him. And though he weighed somewhat less than when he left, he had somehow — in his own eyes and in theirs — grown considerably. His pride in this feeling was evident in one of his comments.

"I used to be so small when everyone else was so big," he told them seriously. "It was like everybody, even Coral and Beth, knew more than I did and there wasn't anything I could say that everybody didn't know already. But now I know a lot of things that *nobody* else knows, don't I?"

He did indeed, and as they gradually fitted Ben's story together in its proper order, the things that had happened to him seemed all the more incredible and they realized only too well that if such a story became publicly known, Ben would never be able to lead any kind of normal life. He would be pointed out ever after as a curiosity, a freak, and be called names like "badger boy" or worse. With school very soon to begin for him, he would become the butt of merciless teasing and he would not be given the chance he needed to fit in with community life here.

The dilemma was solved in a way which Esther could only describe as providential. On the sixth evening after Ben's return, by which time most of his story had been assimilated by the family, two visitors stopped by the residence on Hawk's Hill. One was Doc Simpson — Dr. Richard M. Simpson of North Corners — who had joined in the initial search for Ben and then came back after a day's absence to help the family search for three more days. The other was the Archbishop Peter Matheson of Winnipeg, who had come to pay a visit to his doctor friend in North Corners.

Doc Simpson had given the archbishop more of the particulars of the MacDonald boy's disappearance, of which the clergyman had heard only sketchy details in Winnipeg. Being this close to where the MacDonalds lived, Archbishop Matheson had asked Doc Simpson if he would mind driving him there in his buggy so he could talk with the family and perhaps comfort them to some degree in their loss.

And so the two men had come to visit and were more than astounded to find Ben there. The whole story came out, along with the ramifications of what would occur if ever it became public knowledge. The archbishop sat back and rubbed his chin thoughtfully for a time and then cleared his throat.

"I would not hesitate in the least to say that we have seen here the manifestation of God's hand. This remarkable incident and the change in the child since his return bears all the earmarks of a divine intervention. I do believe it might be termed something of a minor miracle . . . and perhaps not so minor at that. Don't you agree, Richard?"

Doc Simpson nodded, removed the pipe from between his teeth and said, "I couldn't agree with you more. Quite frankly, if it had been hearsay I wouldn't have believed it." He pointed the pipestem at the bedroom where Ben and the badger were sleeping and added, "Suffice to say I'm convinced of it."

The archbishop nodded and continued, directing his remarks to Esther and William MacDonald.

"It is not the purpose of the Church," he said, "to encourage the dissemination of a falsehood, regardless of the good intentions it fosters. Yet, neither is it the purpose of the Church to needlessly and pointlessly inflict harm, mentally or physically."

He paused again to put his thoughts in order and then, choosing his words carefully, continued: "In the three years of His preachment, the Savior told many stories which in those days were called parables. While they might have been true, they were not necessarily so; but neither were they lies in the sense of deliberate and malicious prevarication. They were simply parables: stories told with a point to put across in a more acceptable and meaningful way than by simply stating a fact.

"In your case, Mr. and Mrs. MacDonald, I would say — and I believe the good doctor would second me — that a parable under these circumstances would be more appropriate and, as parables are, more valuable than mere hard facts. This would be the parable of a small lost child caught in the grip of the elements, frightened and bewildered. In some respects like the lost lamb of the shepherd's flock. Now then, Richard," he said, turning toward the doctor again, "since you are familiar with the speech, what is the Indian name for the badger?"

"Several of 'em," Simpson replied, "depending on tribe and dialect. One is *Ith-thay-pootee* and another is *Mittenusk*. Then there's —"

The archbishop raised a hand and stopped him. "That second one will suffice. So, getting back to our parable, we have a little lost boy caught in the elements and in this dire predicament he is found by one named Mittenusk, who shares home and food with him, protects him, watches over him, even adopts him, until at last he can be reunited with his grieving family who, like the good shepherd, have refused to give him up for lost.

"It is a good parable," he said, nodding, "and it is simple, just as an effective parable should be. It also makes a good point: this being that even under the most dreadful of circumstances, there is One who watches over us all and who can and will, given the chance and the belief, protect and preserve us.

"I do not," he cleared his throat again, "say this lightly. It is the foundation of my belief and the rock upon which the Church is built. Providence? Divine intervention? Indeed, I have no doubt of it. Can you conceive of any other way a six-year-old child — unusually small for his age at that — could survive for two months in the vastness of the prairie? True, he survived through the efforts of a badger, a wild animal considered among the fiercest in this land for its size. Who, then, are we to say that a Power far beyond this creature was not directing her; that a

Power far beyond her did not carefully set up the circumstances by which such a miracle could come to pass?"

And so this was how the word of Ben's recovery spread across the Manitoba country. Not unexpectedly, as events of such unusual interest do, the account that was so simple became embellished and "improved upon" until the entire populace was quite convinced that a powerful Blackfoot chief named Mittenusk had been passing through the country with his small band of followers on the day when the little MacDonald boy wandered off and became lost. Chief Mittenusk had, so the story went now, not only saved the boy's life but he had also adopted him as his own son and kept him safe until his band's travels brought them back to this area, whereupon he returned the child to his parents.

There was even an additional and entirely unexpected sidelight to the embellishment. This great Blackfoot chief, so it was whispered, had come to the Winnipeg area seeking vengeance for wrongs done to him and his people by a huge, black-bearded trapper; that this man had not been found but his dog was, and that the dog was captured and slain in a gruesome manner as a sample of what was in store for the trapper. But this was secondary material and for the most part accepted as invention on someone's part. What was primary in the discussion of the people was the fact of Benjamin MacDonald's miraculous return, for which God and Chief Mittenusk were given credit.

For the most part, people respected the announced wishes of the MacDonalds that they wanted no great personal fanfare to be made over Ben. The neighbors were genuinely pleased and happy for the family at the recovery of the boy and they were only too glad that the family was discouraging visitors, since quite a number of them were more embarrassed than ever now for having so quickly given up the search. Yet, there were still a few who came, ostensibly to pay their respects and extend their congratulations, but actually more to see this little child who had undergone such an extraordinary experience.

As for Ben, a trace of his former shyness was still there where strangers were concerned and he remained somewhat reticent about talking much to anyone outside the family; but he did surprise and delight Esther and William MacDonald by gravely shaking hands with the visitors, even if he would not say very much to them. Their pleasure was even greater when Ben exhibited a marked anticipation for his entry into school less than a week from now and the doubts that had assailed them so short a time ago in regard to his readiness for it had now dissolved.

One major problem remained: the badger. Ben was unshakably determined that he would not go to school unless he could take her with him each day. And perhaps it was not even a matter of choice, for the big female badger still showed a strong determination to go wherever Ben went. This was the situation as matters were rapidly spiraling toward a new crisis. But then another visitor came to Hawk's Hill.

His name was George Burton.

Chapter 13

The air was crisp and the sunrise bright with the promise of a glorious day in prospect when George Burton rode up the sloping wagon road on Hawk's Hill to the MacDonald place that first Saturday in September. His rifle was couched in his arms, as he had taken to carrying it ever since Lobo had vanished. Later on it was supposed that he had come to inquire if anyone there — Ben in particular, of course — knew anything about the disappearance of his dog and if the Indians who had rescued the boy were really searching for a bearded white man. But that was only speculation; no one really knew for sure why he came.

The first chores of the morning, begun at dawn, had been finished. The cow had been milked and turned out to pasture, fresh straw had been forked into the horse stalls, and all the livestock seen to and fed. Everyone helped, as usual, even Ben and the girls — Beth and Coral feeding and watering the chickens and feeling in the nest boxes for any early-morning eggs; Ben carrying buckets of water from the new well to the sheep trough.

As she had taken to doing these past few mornings, the female badger stretched out on her stomach at full length on the very peak of the dirt mound by the well, seeming to enjoy the light breeze riffling her long hair as her eyes lazily followed Ben doing his chores. And when Esther had clanged the triangle and the family had all trooped in for breakfast, the badger had remained where she was, dozing as the first warm rays of the sun bathed her.

She had become accustomed to the variety of noises about the farm; the bleating of the sheep, the way the horses nickered and stamped their feet, the clang of metal, thump of wood and creaking of leather, and she was no longer as suspiciously alert as she had been during those first days here. Thus, she paid little attention at first to the sound of approaching hooves, merely twitching an ear but keeping her eyes shut. As they came still nearer, however, she did open them and then she was instantly alert.

The horse was only thirty yards away, turning into the yard, and there was a great bearded man astride the animal. He saw her only a fractional instant before she saw him and both man and animal were galvanized into action. As the badger plunged down the earth pile, Burton flung the rifle to his shoulder and snapped off a shot. The bullet, too hastily aimed, barely nicked her haunch, but with enough force to flip her over just as she reached the bottom of the pile.

Snarling savagely, she regained her feet and began running full tilt for the dark haven beneath the porch.

She didn't make it. The second shot caught her in the side and slammed her heavily against the base of the house. She bounced a little and rolled over onto her back and this time she did not move again.

So quickly had it happened, so unexpectedly, that even though the MacDonald family had jumped to their feet with the first shot, they had not even reached the door when the second shot came. John was first outside and he stopped so suddenly that his father bumped into him. Ben, close behind, skirted around them and glanced toward the dirt pile. He saw her immediately near the corner of the house.

"Badger!" the word erupted from him as a shriek and he leaped off the porch and raced toward her, screaming at each step, "No . . . no . . . no . . ."

MacDonald had seen her and he was running too, but not after his son. He ran toward Burton's horse. The bearded man was grinning, evidently proud of his marksmanship, but as he saw the expression on the farmer's face the grin vanished. His horse shied slightly at the man's approach and MacDonald grasped the bridle with his left hand. He glared at the trapper.

"You idiot!" he thundered. "Give me that gun."

Though taken aback, Burton was not slow to respond. He moved the weapon but rather than handing it over, he pointed it very deliberately at the center of William MacDonald's chest.

"Dunno what's eatin' you, MacDonald," he said

menacingly, "but they ain't no man gonna take my gun. Back off."

MacDonald didn't. Instead he jerked aside, snatched the barrel of the gun with his free hand and let go of the bridle. Simultaneously he swatted the horse's neck and yanked on the weapon. The horse reared in fright and Burton's tight grip on the rifle unseated him. Even as the trapper was pitched from the saddle, the gun fired.

Esther screamed piercingly and John, still standing frozen on the porch, cried, *"Dad!"* Ben was on the ground beside the house, cradling the badger's head in his lap and whimpering as he stared at the men.

The bullet grazed MacDonald's left side, causing him to lurch with pain, but he did not lose his grip on the gun barrel. As Burton struck the ground with a heavy thud on his shoulder and side he was momentarily dazed and lost his hold on it. MacDonald snatched it away, strode to a nearby heavy, iron-wheeled plough and slammed the weapon down across the metal. It broke in half and the splintered stock end came to rest against the far wheel.

"William!"

At Esther's cry he spun around, still gripping the octagonal barrel of the gun. Burton was almost on him and in his hand now he held the dangerous-looking bone-handled skinning knife. MacDonald instinctively swung the mutilated weapon in his grip at Burton's arm, missed it but managed to hit the blade a glancing blow and sent the knife spinning away a dozen feet. But the momentum of the blow had thrown the farmer off balance and before he could recover, Burton's huge fist caught him a powerful thudding blow on the side of the head. The impact dazed MacDonald and he staggered backward, collided with the near wheel of the plough, and fell.

Burton scrambled after the knife, snatched it up and turned back toward the farmer. MacDonald, the side of his shirt now darkly stained with blood, was trying to get to his feet but he couldn't seem to recover his coordination.

The big trapper was closing in when suddenly a heavy weight struck him in the small of the back. It was John, who had sped across the yard and hurled himself bodily at Burton. The bearded man lost the knife again and staggered, but he did not fall. Roaring with anger he struggled with the youth who was holding on to his waist and suddenly he jerked his own arm back. The point of his elbow struck John just over the right eye with the force of a club and John fell flaccidly, face down in the dirt.

Though MacDonald had pulled himself to his feet, he was not yet in full control of himself and was leaning groggily against the wheel of the machine. For the second time Burton scooped up the knife.

The shot came as a complete surprise to him. It struck the ground only a foot in front of him, evidently hit a rock just under the surface and burst upward in a screaming ricochet. Flying dirt sprayed Burton and he froze.

"Drop it! Drop that knife!"

It was Esther. She was white-faced and the barrel of her husband's rifle was shaking in her awkward pointing of it, but it was well enough aimed at this range to terrify Burton. He yelled, "Don't shoot!" and dropped the knife instantly. He had no doubt whatever that she would not hesitate about shooting him.

Reasonably recovered now, MacDonald went to her, skirting widely around Burton and keeping out of her line of aim. The farmer shook his head a time or two to clear his vision and as he neared her she could see that already an enormous bluish lump was forming just in front of his right ear.

"See to John," he said, taking the gun from her. He waved the barrel at Burton. "Move away some," he ordered.

The trapper backed up ten or twelve steps and then stopped. His face had become sickly pale against the black of his beard and he was breathing heavily. As his eyes moved furtively back and forth MacDonald was shocked to realize that the big man was almost hysterically afraid.

John was coming around. He was sitting up by the time Esther reached him and she assisted him to his feet. With her arm around him she helped him walk until they were behind his father. William MacDonald moved up to within ten feet of Burton, the rifle held at his hip and the hole in its muzzle locked on the middle of the trapper's massive chest. The farmer's voice, when he spoke at last, was cold, implacable and imminently deadly.

"Don't talk, Burton, just listen. You've nothing to say that I want to hear. I'm a God-fearing man and I detest violence, but I swear to you now as God is my witness, if you ever set foot on my land again, I'll kill you on sight."

Burton licked his lips and a muscle under his right eye twitched repeatedly, but he said nothing. There was no mistaking the dreadful menace of the man standing before him. After a moment's pause, Mac-Donald continued.

"I want you away from here, Burton. I want you off this land and out of this country. You paid Edgar Cecil three thousand dollars for his place. Since then you've run it down, but that's what I'll pay you. I'll give the money to Doc Simpson tomorrow and you can get it from him. You'll give him the deed, signed over to me. You have no choice. I give you just three days to pack up and clear out. If you're not gone by then, I'll come looking for you; and make no mistake, when I find you, I'll kill you! Now get on your horse and ride out of here."

Moving hesitantly at first but then with fear lending him momentum, Burton backed off and then turned and ran to his horse which was standing thirty yards off. He leaped into the saddle and kicked the horse into a gallop, bending low over the animal's neck as they went, as if he still expected a bullet to come his way. He had stared death in the face and he knew it. Big he might be physically, but he was not now, nor had he ever been, a brave man.

MacDonald watched until the rider was swallowed down the slope of the wagon road. Then he lowered the gun and his shoulders sagged. He walked slowly back toward where Esther and John were still standing. She ran to him, still frightened, and took his arm as he stopped and kissed her forehead.

"It's all right, honey," he murmured. "Everything's all right now."

But not until she had opened his shirt with shaking fingers and saw that his wound was only a superficial trench gouged in the flesh of his side did the paralyzing fear begin to leave her. Now it was she who sagged against him. John came to them and MacDonald smiled and squeezed his shoulder.

"We have another man in the house now, Esther," he said. "Go get that knife, John. It's yours." He looked at his wife with sudden concern. "Where are the girls?"

Esther laughed nervously. "In their room and I wouldn't be surprised if they were under the bed. I sent them there when I went in after the gun." She shuddered. "Do you realize that's the first time I ever fired a gun at anything except a target?"

He chuckled. "After all these years I'm still learning that I married quite a woman."

She blinked rapidly, but then her voice became

brisk. "Come inside so I can wash and dress that wound."

He shook his head and said softly, "Ben first. This'll keep. We'd better see to him."

Ben was still sitting there by the corner of the house with the badger's head in his lap, stroking her. Tears were coursing down his cheeks but he was making no sound. MacDonald squatted in front of him and Esther did likewise. The farmer reached out his hand and stroked the long, grizzled fur. It was the first time he had touched the animal and he could still feel the warmth of it. The badger's eyes were partially open and glazed. The fur of her hip was stained where the first bullet had nicked her, and a crimson blot on each side attested to where the second bullet had gone through her.

"We'll help you bury her, son," he said.

For the first time since he ran to her, Ben moved. He set her head gently on the ground and shook his own head. "I'll do it," he said. "By myself. Out there." He indicated the prairie.

MacDonald was on the point of saying no, but he was stayed by the tightening of Esther's grip on his arm. He nodded faintly to her.

"All right, Ben," he told the boy. "We'll be here if you need us."

Ben watched them as they went into the house. John came up to him with Burton's skinning knife in his hand. He didn't know quite what to say and at last he blurted, "I'm sorry it happened, Ben. Do you want me to help you with her?"

Ben shook his head.

"You want to use this knife to dig with?"

"No!" Ben almost shouted the word and was immediately contrite. "No," he repeated more softly. "I don't want to touch it. I'll make out all right."

When his little brother didn't say anything else, John turned and went up on the porch. At the doorway he paused and looked back. "I'm really sorry, Benjy."

He hadn't called Ben by the nickname in nearly a year and Ben looked up and smiled, strangely touched by it. The expression faded as John went inside. Ben looked at the badger again and his vision swam. Somehow he couldn't seem to stop crying. He wiped his eyes with the heel of his hand but they just filled up again right away. He leaned over and with a fingertip he closed first one of the badger's eyes and then the other.

Close at hand, in the long narrow flower bed his mother kept beside the house, a little hand trowel was stuck in the ground. He reached for it and knocked the dirt off the blade, then slipped it into his waistband. Still on his knees, he slid his hands under the badger's stomach and tried to lift her, but she was too heavy and much too unwieldy for him like this.

Very gently he turned her over onto her back, cupping her shoulders on one forearm and raising her until she was almost in a sitting position. Then he got his other arm under her rump and managed to lift her, cradling her like a baby in his arms. She was not a great deal smaller than himself, nor so very much lighter, and he had great difficulty getting to his feet with her. Then he began to walk unsteadily, staggering much from the heaviness of the animal.

He started off by following the corral fence, as he had followed it on that day he had become lost. He planned to take her back to the burrow and lay her in the den. He would seal the emergency exit from the inside and then go out himself through the main passage and cave it in when he got to the surface. If he got lost again in the process, he didn't care. He didn't care about anything right now. Once or twice as he walked with her a low whining chatter welled up in his throat.

Halfway to the end of the corral fence he knew he couldn't possibly make it. Already his strength was failing and he wouldn't possibly be able to carry her all the way to the den, even assuming he could find the place. He was crying again, harder; crying at his own frailty as well as at his loss.

In a blur ahead of him he could see the south corner of the corral. That was the spot where he had flushed the nesting prairie chicken and she had gone clucking away, dragging her wing and leading him toward his eventual encounter with the animal now in his arms. It would be a fitting place to bury her; there, just beyond the last post, on the southern slope of Hawk's Hill.

For the last ten feet or so he was actually stumbling under her weight and it was only with the greatest of effort that he was able to fall to his knees and set her down gently in the grass. Breathing heavily, he began at once to dig with the garden tool, but suddenly he dropped it and flung himself down at full length beside the badger and buried his face in the soft fur of her stomach. Harsh wailing cries erupted from him and his body was racked by great shuddering sobs.

At length he quieted somewhat and turned his face so that now it was his cheek and the side of his head pressing against her. Then his entire body stiffened and even his breathing stopped. He pressed closer against her and put his hand over his exposed ear so as to hear better with the other.

He *hadn't* imagined it! The sound was there. Rapid and hard to detect, but unmistakably a heartbeat. The badger was still alive!

He raised his head and looked at her. The eyes were open again; not all the way, in fact only a little, but they had opened. A burst of exultation blossomed in him and even while his spirits soared he berated himself for not realizing before this that she was still alive. When he had buried his face in her belly fur, she was warm, not cool as she would have been had she been dead. He should have realized it then!

He leaped to his feet and ran toward the house, only to stop after a dozen yards and run back to her. He couldn't leave her alone this way. With renewed strength he got her back into his arms and began a stumbling shuffle with her toward the house. And at last he found his voice.

"Dad! Dad! Help me. *Dad!*"

He was still calling when they boiled out of the house and came running toward him, his father and John rapidly outdistancing the others. The elder Mac-Donald was bare-chested and a new bandage shone with startling whiteness around his middle.

Gasping, sobbing with relief, the explanation leaped out of Ben in spurts and spasms as they neared.

"She's alive ... Dad ... John ... alive! ... I heard ... it ... Heart ... Heard it beating ... She's warm ... alive ... *alive!*"

He toppled as they reached him and John just managed to reach out and prevent Ben from falling with her. Carefully their father lifted the animal out of Ben's arms and cradled her in his own, then carried her quickly to the house while Ben danced back and forth around him in tremendous excitement. Esther and the girls met them closer to the house and MacDonald nodded.

"She's alive, all right. Just saw her eyes blink. Looks like you're going to have another patient to treat, Esther."

Though he said it seriously enough, it was actually he who doctored her. He laid her on a clean piece of heavy cloth, called for water and medications, and, when they were brought on the run, bathed the wounds on either side with remarkable gentleness.

The entry hole on her left side was only the size of the bullet and, surprisingly, that on the right was very little larger. MacDonald talked ramblingly as he worked over her.

"Clean wound. In and out. May not live, though. No bones hit or the bullet would've spread a lot more." He opened the exit wound with his thumbs, looked carefully in as far as he could, then sniffed it. "No smell of wastes. Must've missed the bowel, too. Lucky. Might make it at that. Just might."

He used whiskey as an antiseptic on the outside of the wounds, but at the faint cringing of the animal at this pain, decided against dampening a swab with the liquor to probe inside. "Better leave well enough alone," he muttered. "There'd be too much shock. Just cleanse the outside. Get my razor, somebody."

Ben got it and brought it back on the run. He handed it to his father and watched as the man shaved a three-inch circle around both wounds, cleaned the openings again with whiskey, gently rubbed a medicating salve on them and then called for bandages. He placed a fresh cloth padding on each side and then firmly but not tightly he wrapped stripping around and around her body until little of either side of her was visible. He also cleaned and medicated the nick on her rump, but did not bandage that wound. Then, with the family at his heels, he gently raised her and carried her into the bedroom where she and Ben had been sleeping and laid her on the matting. The badger sighed and wheezed faintly as he put her down.

As he let go of her, MacDonald felt a touch on his arm and turned, still with one knee on the floor. It was Ben.

"Dad," the boy said hesitantly, "will she live?"

MacDonald felt a sudden strong impulse to be cheerfully optimistic for Ben's sake. The boy had been through so much; why add to his troubles? But then he shook his head slightly. If ever there was a time to be completely honest with his little son, it was at this moment. He reached out and put a hand on Ben's shoulder and again he shook his head.

"I really doubt it, Ben. I don't see how. Even if the bullet didn't hit any vital organs, the shock of it is still apt to kill her. Sometimes animals — and men, too — can survive with terrible wounds, so maybe there's a hope, but I wouldn't count on it. I don't like saying it, but I honestly believe she'll not make it through the night."

Ben's lower lip trembled but he said nothing and MacDonald squeezed his shoulder, wishing there were words he could say to make it easier, wishing there was some way to put across to a little six-year-old that life is such a fragile thing and that, painful though it might be, death is a part of life. Realizing this, accepting it, is a part of growing up. But it was never easy to accept, not for anyone.

"I hope she'll live, Ben," he added softly. It was all he could say.

Ben nodded and though there was a deep pain in his eyes, he met his father's gaze directly. It came as a shock to MacDonald to realize that Ben did understand the unspoken words. The boy's voice was uneven and barely under control when he spoke.

"If she ... dies ... would you help me bury her, Dad?"

MacDonald's own vision began swimming a little and he raised his hand from Ben's shoulder and curled it around the back of the boy's neck. And without even realizing it, he now found exactly the right words.

"Of course, Ben. If she doesn't make it and if you think it's the right thing to do, we'll take her together out to the place where you lived with her and we'll put her there in her den where she belongs for the last time."

A new flood of tears slid down Ben's cheeks and for a long moment he simply looked at his father, sharing with the man a new bond that he had not realized there could be. MacDonald said nothing more and there was an eloquence in their mutual silence.

And then, in a rush, Ben came into his arms. He wrapped his own little arms tightly around his father's neck, sobbing uncontrollably. So fiercely did Ben cling that it almost cut off his father's breath, but William MacDonald didn't mind.

Not at all.